my life after now

JESSICA VERDI

sourcebooks
fire

Published by Sourcebooks Fire, an imprint of Sourcebooks, Inc.
P.O. Box 4410, Naperville, Illinois 60567-4410
(630) 961-3900
Fax: (630) 961-2168
teenfire.sourcebooks.com

Library of Congress Cataloging-in-Publication data is on file with the publisher.

Printed and bound in the United States of America.
VP 10 9 8 7 6 5 4 3 2 1

To Michael,
my inspiring and incredible friend,
and to Paul,
my wonderful and
unfathomably supportive husband

1

Back to Before

The drama club homeroom was buzzing with post-summer chatter, but I didn't look up from my copy of *Romeo and Juliet*. Auditions were this afternoon, and there was no such thing as being too prepared.

I closed the play and ran through the monologue by memory. "O Romeo, Romeo! Wherefore art thou Romeo?" I whispered to myself, my long hair hanging like blackout curtains around my face. I got so into it that it wasn't until I got to the part about *it is not hand, nor foot, nor arm, nor face, nor any other part belonging to a man* that I realized I was no longer whispering. I giggled and looked around quickly, embarrassed. But the only person who seemed to be paying me any attention was Ty. My beautiful, talented boyfriend.

"What part of a man might you be referring to, my dear Juliet?" he teased, a dark eyebrow raised.

"Why, the ears, of course," I said, all innocence. He laughed and put an arm around me. I snuggled into him and promptly turned my attention back to my work.

Ty was a senior, the president of the drama club, and one of the club's few straight male members. He'd been the leading man in every Eleanor Drama production for the past three years, and the leading man in my life for the past year and a half. We were each other's firsts—when it came to pretty much everything. I'd never even kissed a boy offstage before Ty.

Andre, our director, called the homeroom to attention. "Good morning, all you gorgeous thespians!" he said, clasping his hands together dramatically. Andre spent what he called his "sexy years"—aka the 1980s—in the New York theater scene. Eight shows a week for five years, he wore the now-iconic jazzercise unitard and striped face makeup in *Cats*. But it wasn't until after his five-performance run in the chorus of the ill-fated *Carrie* that he quit and shifted his attention to directing. "So many new faces, so much fresh talent," he said with an approving nod. "Welcome to Eleanor Drama, everyone!"

I glanced around the room. Andre was right—there *were* a lot of new people in the club this year. And anyone who'd watched the local news or picked up a newspaper at all in the last month knew why.

What happened was, three towns over from my hometown of Eleanor Falls, some moronic nineteen-year-old on the five-year plan thought it would be hilarious to plant a homemade bomb in his high school gym. It went off at three a.m. in the middle of August, so no one was hurt, but Brighton High was officially closed. Which left the school's administration scrambling to place their eighteen hundred high school students before the start of the school year.

The athletes were sent to the districts with the best sports programs, the science kids went to the schools with the nicest lab facilities, and the drama and music kids came here. Eleanor Senior High.

Eleanor's performing arts department was well known across the lower half of New York State. Our state-of-the-art auditorium was often compared to a Broadway theater, and our drama program produced *fifteen* alumni in the last twelve years who had gone on to Juilliard.

The only problem was the new kids included Elyse St. James. The world's most loathsome, repellent, horrid excuse for a—

"Lucy, why don't you go next?" Andre said to me, snapping me out of my reverie. We were doing dumb introductions, and it was my turn.

"Hi, everyone," I said. "I'm Lucy Moore, I'm a junior, and my favorite show is *Rent*."

My lifelong best friends Courtney and Max named their favorite shows as *Pygmalion* and *The Rocky Horror Show*, respectively, which tells you pretty much everything you need to know about them, and Ty quoted *Twelve Angry Men* as his. Apart from the five Brighton transfers, the new additions included the three lucky freshmen who'd actually made it past Andre's rigorous audition process and a senior named Evan who'd just moved here from California.

And then it was *her* turn. Elyse and I had competed for the female leads in every Proscenium Pines theater camp summer production since fifth grade. She was one of those musical theater princesses you see at auditions in the city who show up with rollers in their hair and wear character shoes with their dresses even if it's a nondancing audition.

Oh, and Elyse St. James was *not* her real name. Well, I guess it was now, since she'd had it legally changed, but when I first met "Elyse," her name was Ambrosia Burris. Yes. Seriously.

And let's just say her name wasn't the only "augmented" thing about her.

"Hello, I'm Elyse St. James," she trilled. "I'm *so* excited to be starting my junior year at Eleanor—I've wanted to be part of this drama program for a long time." She flashed Andre a kiss-up smile with unnaturally pink, glossed lips. "Oh, and my favorite play of all time"—she looked straight at me when she said this next part—"is *Romeo and Juliet.* I'm really looking forward to this afternoon's audition."

"That's great, Elyse. I'm sure you'll make a really great Nurse," I replied sweetly.

She shot me daggers from her perfectly lined eyes.

"Let the games begin," Max muttered under his breath.

• • •

Two days later, the cast list was posted, as follows:

Romeo: Ty Parker
Juliet: Elyse St. James
Nurse: Kelly Ortiz
Capulet: Max Perry

Lady Capulet: Courtney Chen

Montague: Christopher Mendoza

Lady Montague: Bianca Elizabeth Glover

Mercutio: Lucy Moore

Tybalt: Evan Davis

Benvolio: Nathan Pittman-Briggs

Prince Escalus: Isaac Stein

Count Paris: Dominick Ellison

Friar Laurence: Violet Patel

Ensemble (from which the roles of Chorus, Peter, Sampson, Petruchio, Gregory, Abraham, Balthasar, Friar John, and the Apothecary, among others, are to be cast): Jonathan Poole, Andrea Wong, Stephanie Gilmore, Marti Espinoza, Stephen Larson

My eyes were playing tricks on me.

I closed them, rubbed my lids, opened them again. The list hadn't changed.

But that role was *mine*. Andre had promised. Okay, maybe he hadn't *promised*, but he'd sure *hinted* a hell of a lot. I mean, what else was the phrase, "I chose this play with you in mind, Lucy," accompanied by a wink and smile, supposed to mean?

I looked around, panicked, for Ty. I needed him—he would make it all make sense. But I didn't see him anywhere, and the reality of the casting was sinking in fast.

My mouth had gone dry and my legs were beginning to tremble. Courtney and Max shared a worried glance and quickly guided me into the girls' bathroom. That's when I really broke down.

"I *hate* her! That fake, stupid cow! Why did she have to come here? She's ruining *everything*!"

My friends just sat on the cold tile floor beside me and held my hands and rubbed my back, letting me get it all out. I had a sudden flash of the last time they'd comforted me like this, three years ago—but the memory was interrupted when a cluster of freshman girls walked into the restroom. They stopped when they saw us.

"Hey, you're not supposed to be in here," one girl whined to Max.

"Like I care about your girly business," he said, rolling his eyes.

The girl eyed his sassy wax-molded hair and his green slim-fit cardigan over his Lady Gaga t-shirt, and her face clicked with understanding. Then she pointed to me. "So what's the matter with her, anyway?"

"Don't worry about it," Max said.

The girls stared at me, still going to pieces, a second more. Then they just shrugged and left.

"Guess they didn't have to pee after all," Max muttered, and brushed my hair away from my face.

When my sobs had died down to a whimper, Courtney spoke. "Lucy, sweetie, the read-through is going to start in a couple minutes. You gonna go?"

I looked at her and then at Max. They smiled unsurely back at me. I knew them well: they wanted to be supportive but were also ready to get the hell out of the bathroom and to rehearsal. Suddenly I felt bad; I couldn't keep them in here any longer. So I nodded, stood on shaky legs, and splashed cool water on my face. "Sorry, guys," I said, starting to feel a little embarrassed by my reaction.

"It's okay. We think Elyse is a fake, stupid cow too."

I managed a tiny laugh. Max always knew what to say to make me feel better.

"I know you probably don't want to hear this," Courtney said as we walked to rehearsal, "but Mercutio is a pretty awesome role. You're going to rock it."

I sighed. I usually loved that Andre was all about the nontraditional casting. And Mercutio really was a great part. But I'd had my heart set on Juliet.

The second we entered the auditorium, Andre pulled me aside. In the darkness of the unlit house, slumped in the very last row of seats, I only half listened to his explanation. He fed me some obviously rehearsed crap about wanting to give me a role that would *challenge* me, and how he gave Elyse the lead because it was a safe part, and she was a safe actor. It was all total BS, of course.

"Whatever, Andre. Just admit that you gave her the role because you thought she would do a better job than I would."

Silence. Andre stared straight ahead, his unfocused gaze resting on the cast doing warm-up exercises up on the stage.

"Please," I said.

Andre sighed. "She gave a great audition…"

"Just say it." I didn't know why, but I needed to hear the words.

"Okay, fine." He twisted his fingers around each other uneasily. "I gave her the role because I thought she would do a better job than you."

And there it was. The honest truth. For all my hard work and preparation, I still wasn't good enough.

Don't get me wrong—I knew that I wasn't going to get every role I ever auditioned for. I'd even lost roles to Elyse before, at theater camp. But this was different. This was *my* school, *my* drama club, *my* life. I'd always been the star of my own little corner of the world—landing all the best parts since freshman year, getting straight As even in my advanced classes, finding out that the first guy I ever really liked actually liked me back. But then Elyse came along, and in one fell swoop things suddenly weren't so easy anymore.

And that was only my first problem.

2

Forget About the Boy

As I walked away from Andre, I made the split-second decision that I was going to convince everyone that I was fine—no, *thrilled*—with the way things turned out. No way was I going to give Elyse the satisfaction of knowing that she'd gotten under my skin.

So when Ty wrapped his arms tightly around me and whispered, "Are you okay?" in my ear, I gave a little laugh and assured him that I was actually glad to have a role that I could experiment with and truly make my own. I must have been really convincing because he kissed me and said, "Lucy, you are a true actor. Believe me, if I hadn't gotten Romeo, I wouldn't be nearly as understanding as you." He ruffled my hair and then leapt up on the stage in one bound, taking his place in the read-through circle.

See, Andre? I thought bitterly, *I am a good actor.*

But soon even I was having trouble believing that. I'd only paid attention to Juliet's part during the summer, and it felt wrong to suddenly be speaking Mercutio's words. They were foreign to me and clunked around in my mouth like marbles. While Elyse breezed through the complicated Shakespearean language like it was her favorite song, I stumbled and fell over each line.

And, on top of everything else, she had taken to flirting with Ty. She wasn't even discreet about it. Playful touches on his arm, whispers in his ear, giggling like a maniac every time he said anything even remotely amusing. Right in front of me. All afternoon.

If it hadn't been clear that Ty was completely uninterested in her, I would have given up on my vow to remain upbeat. It was like she was on a mission to steal my life.

I got home that night to find that my dads had left a dozen pink roses waiting for me on the kitchen table. The card read: *A rose by any other name…Congratulations, Lucy!* I plunked myself down in a kitchen chair, the sweet aroma filling my nose, and couldn't help but smile. My dads were probably the only two gay men in the world who knew nothing about theater. I knew the only reasons they'd chosen that line were because it had to do with flowers, which was one stereotypical gay interest they actually did subscribe to, and my middle name was Rose. But their well-meaning clue-lessness actually cheered me up a little.

I went into the living room, where Dad and Papa were curled up on the sofa in their matching Snuggies, watching *The West Wing* on DVD. Mine were the only parents of anyone I knew who were not only still together, but actually still in love.

"Thanks for the flowers," I said, squeezing in between them.

"So?" Papa said, passing me the popcorn bowl. "Are we looking at Eleanor Senior High's new Juliet?"

"Alas, you are not," I said.

Dad paused the TV. "What happened?"

"Elyse St. James happened."

"Oh, honey. I'm so sorry," Dad said. That's another thing I loved about my parents. They may not have cared about theater, but they cared that *I* cared about theater. "What part did you get?"

"Mercutio." I shrugged. "At least I still get to die onstage."

· · ·

The next morning, I got to my locker to find it covered in pictures. Printouts from the Internet of random actors: Laurence Olivier, Keanu Reeves, Ben Affleck, John Barrymore, the guy who played Michael on *Lost*. All artfully arranged so that not an inch of the slate gray locker surface showed.

I stared at the collage, dumbfounded. Who put it there? What did it mean?

"What do you think?" Ty's voice said, close to my ear.

I whirled around. "Did *you* do this?"

He stuck his hands in his pockets and leaned back on his heels, a proud look on his face. "Yup. Got here early and everything."

"But…*why?*" It didn't come out right. I meant it as a genuine question—I was totally confused—but it sounded like I was accusing him of something.

11

Ty's grin melted. "You hate it. I knew it was a stupid idea." He moved to tear the pictures down, but I blocked his path.

"I don't hate it. I just don't understand it."

"They're all pictures of famous people who have played Mercutio," he explained. "Max seemed to think you were pretty upset about not getting Juliet. I told him you seemed fine to me, but he insisted. So I thought it might make you feel better to see that you're in good company."

I turned back to the locker and looked at it again. Of course. John Barrymore played Mercutio in the 1930s movie version of *Romeo and Juliet*. The guy from *Lost* was in the Claire and Leo movie. Laurence Olivier probably played the role on stage—he was in pretty much every Shakespeare play at some time or another.

I reached for Ty's hand and squeezed it tightly. "Thank you," I whispered.

• • •

Two weeks went by. And slowly, I actually started to enjoy playing Mercutio. The role *was* pretty awesome—in the span of only four scenes, I was going to get to be funny, sexy, crude, and violent. And I was going to be killed in a swordfight.

What's in a name? That which we call a rose by any other name would smell as sweet. My dads actually may have unwittingly been onto something with that line, and I kept going back to it in my thoughts. *It doesn't matter what something is called,* I reminded myself, *it matters what something* is. I might not be Juliet, but that didn't mean I couldn't still be great.

Another unexpected upshot of my being cast as Mercutio was that I became friendly with the new guy Evan, who was playing Tybalt. Just by looking at him, you would never guess that he was interested in theater. He wore a baseball cap over his shaggy product-free hair, sported the same faded jeans almost every day, and played video games on his PSP during breaks. But he'd apparently been some sort of stage combat guru at his old drama club, so I guess I lucked out that he was the one who'd be killing me.

Together, we ventured to the massive basement prop room in search of swords. It took a while—we had to squeeze past large backdrops that seemed to have just been thrown into the first available spaces their set-strikers had found and toss aside sheets that were draped over the larger furniture pieces. But when we finally found the swords, we both went motionless, astounded by the sight before us.

"We've hit the mother lode," Evan whispered.

Andre had warned us that there was a ton of swords down here because of a considerable prop donation after the local Renaissance Faire had gone belly-up a couple of years ago, but nothing could have prepared us for this. The prop room was stockpiled with swords in every size and variety imaginable, and they were everywhere. Propped up in rows five layers deep against the walls, sticking up out of large, cylindrical bins, even dangling from racks attached to the ceiling like silver chandeliers.

"Where do we even start?" I marveled.

A slow smile spread across Evan's face. "Anywhere."

I seized a sword at random from the nearest bin and stabbed the air. It felt too light, flimsy. I tried another. This one was painted black and didn't catch the light the way I wanted. I kept choosing swords and they kept letting me down. "How will I even know when I find the right one?" I mumbled.

Evan looked at me in total seriousness. "The right one will find you," he said.

"What is this, Ollivander's Wand Shop?"

Evan stared at me, an unreadable expression on his face.

"What, you've never read *Harry Potter*?" I said.

He laughed. "Of course I have."

"So what's with the—" But I was cut off by the sight of two swords lying side-by-side, individually sheathed in velvet, and resting in their own clear plastic case. I carefully took one from its wrappings. As soon as my palm closed around the silver handle I knew I'd found it.

Evan picked up the other one, and I thought I heard a tiny gasp escape his throat.

These swords were the real thing, with sharp edges, not the blunt kind usually used in theatrics. The weight of it felt good in my hands, made me feel strong. I thrust my sword out at Evan and he immediately responded in kind. The instant the glistening metal collided, an almost indiscernible spark ignited and a pitch-perfect clang reverberated in our ears. Evan and I met each other with matching grins. We were sold.

We both thought it was weird that the school even had the swords at all, but they were amazing and we both loved them. So we agreed that we wouldn't tell Andre.

From that day on, for a half hour at the beginning of every rehearsal, Evan and I worked on choreographing the fight. I couldn't have asked for a better sparring partner—the guy was a fencing *genius*.

"I think he's sexy," Max said one day as he, Courtney, and I watched him from across the auditorium.

"Sorry, Max-a-million," I said. "I'm pretty sure he's straight."

He sighed. "Of course. All the good ones are either straight or taken. Or both." He jerked a thumb at Ty, who was up on the stage learning how to climb up Juliet's balcony. His dancer's body moved lithely, and a little shot of love radiated inside me as I watched him work.

Courtney smacked Max teasingly on the side of the head. "You're crazy. A lack of gay guys is one thing this drama club does not have. It's not *their* fault you're just not interested in any of them." She sighed. "I, on the other hand, really do have a tragic shortage of romantic prospects. At this rate, I'm going to be a forty-year-old virgin."

I laughed. "What about Evan?" I asked, already plotting. "He's kind of my friend now. Want me to ask him if he's into you?" Short, shy, brace-face Courtney was entirely inexperienced when it came to guys. For as long as I'd known her, the only thing she'd ever wanted was to find her Prince Charming.

But she shook her head. "Drama club relationships are way too incestuous. And knowing me, it won't work out, and then we'll be all awkward at rehearsal every day. No thanks."

"Hey, not *all* drama club relationships are a bad idea," I said.

But I soon understood all too well what she'd meant. Cue problem number two.

It was a Sunday afternoon and I was sitting on my bedroom floor, attempting to pick out a Taylor Swift song on my guitar, when I got a text from Courtney:

Look at Elyse's Facebook profile ASAP.

I signed on to the site for the first time in weeks, pulled up Elyse's page, and tried to make sense of the words before me.

♥ **Elyse St. James** is *in a relationship* with **Ty Parker.**

I called Courtney.

"Did you see it?"

"I'm looking at it right now," I said. "You know, I actually feel kinda bad for her. She must have a major inferiority complex if she feels the need to lie about having a boyfriend."

"Lucy," Courtney said slowly, "Facebook doesn't just let you say that you're in a relationship with whoever you want—the other person has to confirm it before the update goes public."

Wait. That was true. But it didn't make sense—why the hell would Ty give her permission to post that? Slowly, a new picture formed in my mind. A more ominous one.

"Lucy? You there?" Courtney asked.

"I gotta go," I whispered. I hung up and immediately called Ty.

He answered on the first ring. "Hey, babe!"

"Do you have anything you want to tell me?" I said.

"What do you mean?"

"According to Elyse's Facebook page, you two are in a *relationship*?"

There was a long pause.

"Ty?" I said softly.

"I didn't think you would see that," he said. "You're never on Facebook."

"What the hell is that supposed to mean?"

He let out a long sigh. "I swear I didn't mean for it to happen," he said. "I didn't even like her in that way."

"You didn't mean for *what* to happen?"

Another pause. Ty didn't want to continue this conversation—that was painfully clear—but finally he spoke. "Last Saturday we were at her house, working on the…more romantic scenes. And I don't know how it happened, but at some point it changed from a stage kiss to a…real kiss."

You have got *to be kidding me,* was all I could think. I knew the difference between stage kisses and real kisses. "So you're telling me there was tongue."

"Yes."

"And…emotions."

"Yes."

"Was it just kissing, or was there anything else? I'm just trying to get the full picture here."

Ty hesitated again. "There may have been some…touching. Over the clothes only," he added, like that made it somehow better.

"Is it still going on?"

"Yes," he said quietly.

"When were you going to tell me?" I asked, trying to keep my voice steady, despite the tears that were silently running down my face.

"I don't know. I guess I was waiting for the right moment."

I hung up without another word.

3

Send in the Clowns

One of the best conversations of my life, one year earlier:

Ty: (floating on an inner-tube in his pool) My sister's getting married.

Me: (sitting on the pool's edge, dangling my feet in the water) Really?

Ty: Yeah. She announced it last night. The wedding's gonna be on New Year's Eve, in the city.

Me: That's amazing!

Ty: Wanna go?

Me: (blinking in surprise) With you? To your sister's wedding?

Ty: Yeah.

Me: (giddy with excitement) Yes! Yes yes yes! But…are you sure you won't change your mind? New Year's is over five months away…

Ty: (pulling me into the water, close to him) Of course I'm sure. I love you, Lucy.

Me: *Gasp!*

Ty: (kisses me passionately)
Me: (grinning like a crazy person) I love you too.
End scene.

There were a lot of awful things about breaking up with Ty, but one of the worst was having to tell people. Because you can't just tell them that you and your boyfriend of a year and half with whom you were never anything but happy are suddenly not together anymore and leave it at that. They want to know why. And it's really embarrassing to admit to your parents and friends that you were cheated on.

Word spread fast. I told Max and Courtney what happened, and they immediately told everyone else. They weren't gossiping—they just wanted to make sure everyone was fully informed, so everyone would take my side. It did seem to work—I noticed people giving Elyse a wide berth and throwing her dirty looks during all nonperforming moments. But it was hard to feel victorious when I was being pitied. If one more person asked me how I was doing or told me what a d-bag they thought Ty was, I was going to scream.

To make matters worse, Ty would not stop apologizing. But there was a caveat: he was only apologizing for the way I found out, not for having cheated. The distinction was not lost on me.

I tried to believe Max and Courtney's words of support—that I was better off without him, that I deserved better—but I couldn't help holding out hope that he would realize his mistake and want me back.

But then I saw them kiss.

We were all gathering up on the stage at the start of rehearsal, and it was impossible to miss the way Ty's face lit up when Elyse entered the room. They ran over to each other like they hadn't seen each other in years, and I watched, powerless, as he cupped her face in his hands and leaned down to kiss her, the way he always used to do with me. The sting I felt at witnessing that was a hundred times worse than the hypothetical mental image of the two of them in her room that had been on a constant loop in the back of my head.

After that, all hope was gone. I ran home and threw away every single memento of our time together. Pictures still in the frames, the favors from his sister's wedding, the dried corsage from his junior prom. I deleted every photo of him from my phone and blocked him on Facebook.

But I couldn't delete him from my mind. Especially since I had to watch him and her being all Romeo and Juliet-y in rehearsals every single day. It was torture.

Elyse herself never said a thing to me. But the smugness was seeping out of her pores. I'd never wanted to punch anyone as badly as I wanted to punch her right in her perfect little surgically-altered nose.

• • •

I came home after rehearsal Friday and went directly to the kitchen on a quest for comfort food. I deserved to overdo it on the calories—pressing pause on the actor diet was my reward for making it through the week from hell. Well, that and a glorious weekend free of Elyse St. Life Destroyer.

I slathered two pieces of bread with butter and added three slices of artificial cheese product. The skillet sizzled and hissed, and I stood in front of the stove, hypnotized, as the flame warmed my face and the gooey orange stuff melted over the crusts. My mouth was actually beginning to water when I heard Dad's voice coming from the living room. That was weird. My dads usually had their date nights on Fridays.

"Lu?" he called to me. "Can you come in here for a minute?"

I flicked the burner off and went into the living room. "What's up?"

And then I saw her. Problem number three.

Lisa Williams was lounging in the big red armchair, legs crossed, looking like she actually thought she belonged there. She flashed a crooked grin at me. I glanced at my fathers over on the couch. Dad had a strained smile on his face, and Papa looked like his head was about to explode. I knew how he felt.

"What's she doing here?"

"Aw, that's no way to treat your dear old mum," she said.

"You are *not* my mother," I snapped, refusing to look at her.

If only that were true.

See, Dad, aka Adam Moore, went through a bit of a "finding himself" phase his last year at Columbia, where he was studying Art History. He had a brief affair with his female best friend, Lisa, and bam, Lisa got pregnant. She was on a student visa from the

U.K., planning on becoming a traveling rock photographer, and not too keen on the idea of having a kid. But Dad, his hetero experimental period all but over, knew it might be his only chance to have a biological child without employing a surrogate. So they made a deal—if Lisa carried me for nine months and gave birth to me, Dad would take over from there. They both upheld their ends of the bargain. For three years, while Dad got his art dealing career started, he and I lived with his parents in Brooklyn. Then Dad met Papa, aka Seth Freeman, attorney-at-law, we moved to our five-bedroom house in Eleanor Falls, Seth legally adopted me, and our family was complete.

I never wondered "where I came from" like most adopted or single-parent kids. My dads were always so forthcoming with information about Lisa that I rarely had any questions. One of my earliest memories was of a much-smaller me sitting on Dad's lap, looking through pictures of the beautiful woman with hair so red and long that it looked aflame, and realizing for the first time that my auburn hair was an exact blend of Lisa's red and Dad's brown locks.

But being fully informed about my mother's identity didn't prevent me from missing her. Every year, we sent Lisa holiday cards and my school photos. I loved going to the post office and telling them we were sending the letter overseas. It made me feel important, special. I always hoped the mail lady would bring me my very own letter from England, stamped with the Queen's face, but that never happened. The first time I heard anything from Lisa was when I was eight years old and she showed up, unannounced, on our doorstep.

At first I didn't believe that she was the same woman from the photos. She was incredibly thin, her hair now a dull orange, her face hollow. She said she'd been back in New York for about a year, and she needed money. She said she had nowhere else to go. She stayed with us for two days. She slept in our guest room, ate our food, used our shower. She didn't hug me or ask about my best subject in school. Her blue eyes darted around nervously, never resting on anything, even me—*especially* me—for longer than a second. And then she left, with cash in her purse and a promise to stay in touch. We didn't hear from her again for five years.

The second time she turned up, she again materialized at our house with no warning. But this time she seemed a lot more put-together—she was wearing makeup and looked a lot healthier. She didn't ask for money—she said she just wanted to get to know me. This time, my dads deferred to me—did I want Lisa to stay with us again? This was my chance—I was thirteen and growing breasts and had recently gotten my period, and the idea of having a mother around was incredibly appealing. I nodded shyly, and Lisa moved in. And it was great. I took her to see my favorite Broadway shows and played her the songs I was learning in my guitar lessons. She told me stories about traveling around Europe and Asia and North America with rock bands. We went shopping and got pedicures. I even introduced her to Max and Courtney.

And then one day, after she'd been living with us for about a month, she was gone. She left a note on the kitchen counter saying that this was all too much too fast and that this life was not what she wanted for herself. I cried myself to sleep for weeks.

And now here she was, sitting in my living room for the third time in my life.

"What is she doing here?" I asked again.

"Lucy," Dad said, "why don't you sit down?"

"Just answer my question."

"Well," Dad said cautiously, "Lisa has asked if she can stay with us for a little while, and I think we should all sit down and discuss our feelings on the subject."

I felt like the wind had been knocked out of me. I couldn't deal with this right now.

"I'm going to spend the night at Courtney's," I said, and ran upstairs.

I logged onto my laptop and three-way Skyped Courtney and Max. "We're going out tonight," I declared.

4
Out Tonight

"I'm going method, guys. For the rest of the night, Lucy Moore will cease to exist." I held up my fake ID. "Tonight, I am Samantha Porter, twenty-two-year-old college student from Philadelphia."

It was nine p.m., and we were on the Metro-North train, barreling toward New York City. Max and I both told our parents that we were sleeping at Courtney's—which we did plan to do eventually, but not until close to dawn. Courtney's mom worked nights at the hospital.

"What brought on this sudden sense of adventure, Luce?" Max asked. We were more of a play-going, movie-renting, coffee-shop-frequenting kind of group. We weren't exactly clubbers. The only reason we even had fake IDs at all was because, continuing with a long-standing Eleanor Drama tradition, last year's seniors had passed them down to us after graduation.

"Are you talking to me?" I asked pointedly. "My name isn't Luce. It's Samantha."

Courtney and Max rolled their eyes in unison. But it got them off my back. They had no idea that Lisa was back, and I wasn't about to talk about it. Tonight I was vacating my life.

"Whatever you say, *Samantha*," Max said.

We got to the club in Chelsea at ten o'clock, ready to dance our feet off, only to find out that they didn't even open until midnight. My heart sank. Probably should have done my research a little better.

"Now what?" Courtney asked.

I held my head high. "Now we just find someplace better to go."

We walked for a while, until we came upon a place that looked promising. There was a velvet rope and an enormous bouncer outside, and there was live music escaping through the open door. I took the lead and confidently flashed my Pennsylvania ID. The bouncer looked at it, chuckled, and shook his head. He knew it was a fake. But I couldn't let him send us away. At this rate, the night was never even going to begin.

I stuck out my boobs and flashed him a coy smile. "Is there a problem, sir?" I asked sweetly.

The bouncer looked me up and down—my hair was tumbling past my shoulders, and I was a vixen in all black: dressed in a low-cut tight tank top, tight jeans, and ankle boots with a stiletto heel. I'd bought the boots for a theater camp production of *Cabaret*, but tonight was the first time I'd ever worn them in real life. To my amazement, the outfit did the trick—he handed the ID back to me, stamped our hands, and waved us inside without even asking Max and Courtney for their IDs.

"That was incredible!" Courtney said as we made our way to the bar. "I thought we were goners for sure."

I bought three Long Island iced teas and slurped mine down before my friends had even finished half of theirs. I promptly ordered another one.

"Um, you okay, Luce?" Max asked me. I wasn't usually much of a drinker.

"*Samantha*," I insisted, pointing to my chest. I finished my second drink and slammed the glass down on the bar. "Let's dance!" I shouted, and began to move to the music.

"Lu—Samantha—I don't think this is the kind of place you dance at," Courtney said.

She was probably right. The band up on the stage was playing acoustic alternative rock, and the most anyone was doing was moving their heads or swaying the tiniest bit in their seats. But the drinks were strong, and my body was warm, and I didn't care what anyone else was doing. I wanted to *dance*. So I did.

And guess what? Other people followed my lead. Soon there were at least a dozen people out of their seats and dancing. After a few songs, the band's lead singer spoke to the crowd.

"We're going to mix things up a little for you guys. This next song is for the girl in black." He pointed to me.

He switched from an acoustic guitar to an electric one, and the band started playing a new song. It was loud and it was fast and it was the best dancing song *ever*.

"Woooo!!!" I screamed, jumping up and down. I wanted another drink, but I didn't want to waste time at the bar, so I just grabbed Max's drink out of his hand and chugged it down. My head was beginning to get fuzzy and spinny. But that was exactly what I wanted. I wasn't able to think about anything but the music.

Courtney and Max joined in at last, and the three of us danced the night away.

After the band's first set, the singer came over to get a drink from the bar. He was gorgeous—flawless hair, totally sexy stubble, vintage tee that showed off the tattoos on his perfect arms. I was shocked as all hell when he approached me.

"Your band rocksss," I slurred.

"Thanks." He grinned and extended his hand to me. "I'm Lee."

"I'm Lucy," I said. *Crap. Samantha. Oh well, too late now.* I made sure to wipe my sweaty hand on my jeans before I shook his.

"You gonna stick around for the next set, Lucy?"

"Absolutely."

"Cool," he said, and hopped back up onto the stage.

Courtney, Max, and I stared after him.

"That is one beautiful man," Max said.

"Amen," Courtney said.

I didn't say anything. I just watched Lee retune his guitar, a smile playing at my lips, knowing I'd just found a surefire way to forget all about Ty.

• • •

One incredible set list and three tequila shots later, Lee found me again, his guitars slung over his back.

"Hey Lucy," he said. "Wanna get out of here?"

I giggled. I'd thought people only said that in the movies. I nodded.

I got up to leave, but Courtney grabbed my arm. "Lucccy, wait...you sssure y'wanna go withhim?"

I laughed. "You're so drunk!" That was the only answer I gave her. Max didn't say anything because he was passed out on the table.

I took Lee's arm, and together we left the club.

5

If My Friends Could See Me Now

A beam of warm, white light pierced my eyelids. I cracked one eye open, then the other, and blinked at the curtainless, bar-clad window.

Where am I?

I moved to prop myself up on my elbows, but the sudden shift in position made my body angry. My stomach heaved and I was weak and shaky. My brain felt like it was sloshing around in my head and crashing into the walls of my skull.

Then I remembered—I got wasted last night. This must be what a hangover felt like. All I could do was lie perfectly still, clear my mind, and wait for the nausea to subside.

When I was ready to try again, I carefully sat up and looked around.

I was in a small room, not much larger than the bed I was in. The sink was piled high with dirty dishes, and laid out on the counter were tiny little Ziploc baggies, needles, and pipes.

Under the unfamiliar sheets, I was completely naked.

I quickly pulled the top sheet up to my chin. The equally-as-naked, tattooed man lying face down beside me sparked a few more sparse fragments of last night. The club. The band. The singer. What was his name? Lee something. Through the filter of my drunken stupor, both he and his apartment had seemed a lot more glamorous last night. But now everything about this place felt dirty.

I shouldn't be here. I have to go home.

As smoothly and quietly as I could manage, I slipped out of bed and gathered my clothes. I dressed quickly, found my purse on the stovetop, and crept out of the apartment, my boots still in my hand.

The door clicked shut behind me, and I leaned against it, my heart racing. My mind was going in a million different directions, but I forced myself to be pragmatic.

First things first: shoes. Gingerly, I sat down on the stairs and wedged my boots on.

Next: communication. I checked my phone. Eight missed calls and seven texts received from Court and Max between one a.m. and six a.m.—which was less than an hour ago. All were various versions of: Where are you? and Are you ok??

I didn't know the answers to either of those questions, but I quickly wrote back, Yeah. Sorry. Explain later. I slid the phone back into my bag.

Next on the agenda: leave this godforsaken place. But my body wouldn't budge. I planted my feet squarely on the step below me and tried again. Nothing. *Come on, body,* I begged. *Work with me here. I promise I'll never do this to you ever again.* I gripped the railing and pressed firmly on the cinderblock wall. Leverage. *Okay,* I warned myself, *on the count of three...*

One.

Two.

Three.

My unwilling body remained stationary. But the alcohol inside it lurched into motion, and before I could do anything to stop it, I was vomiting all over the landing. When I thought there couldn't possibly be anything left in me, another surge came on. I sat there, helpless and miserable, puking my guts out for a long time. At least it was early enough that no one came out of their apartments to find me. Thank god for small favors.

Eventually, the nausea receded. But I was still too brittle to move. I was beginning to think I'd be stuck here forever. Doomed to spend eternity in this filthy stairwell, with no company except a coagulating puddle of puke and some mysterious-looking mold, staring at the outside of Lee's apartment door. I rested my head on the railing.

What happened last night?

I desperately tried to recall even the smallest shard of a memory, some clue as to the events of the last seven hours. But it was hopeless—I couldn't even remember coming to this apartment building, let alone what happened after I got here.

But the longer I sat, the more my head unclogged, and soon a solitary ray of recognition broke through, dull at first but growing sharper. I didn't need to actually remember it to know what had happened; it was obvious from the moment I woke up in that bed. I had sex with Lee.

I suddenly felt an entirely different kind of sick. I drove myself upright at long last and ran down the stairs as fast as I could, not caring about my body's protests and not caring if I woke up the whole building with my clomping. I pushed through the front door, and the cool morning air slapped me in the face. I shivered. My skimpy outfit had seemed like such a good idea last night, but now I just felt foolish and cold.

I rubbed my arms and began to walk. The streets were nearly empty at this hour. I walked briskly, eager to get home, desperate to put as much distance between myself and Lee as possible.

I passed subway stations, and vacant taxis passed me. I had money in my purse—I could have taken any of them. But I welcomed the discomfort that came with walking. The frigid air, the way my stomach lurched with each step I took, the fuzziness of my teeth, the blisters my boots were rubbing into my feet…I deserved all of it and more.

I was filled with shame. Lee was only the second person I'd ever done it with, and I didn't even *remember* it. I knew nothing about him. What was his last name? How old was he? What color were his eyes? Did he treat me nicely?

Soon, Grand Central loomed ahead. I took the first train out of there.

MY LIFE AFTER NOW

Courtney answered the door in her pajamas. Her lips were dry, her long black hair was tangled, and there were dark circles under her eyes. She looked as bad as I felt. "Lucy, thank god! We were so worried!" She pushed me in the direction of the bathroom. "Hurry up and wash your face and put on your pajamas—my mom is gonna be home any minute."

I did as she said and crawled into her enormous bed beside a conked-out Max.

"What happened last night?" Courtney asked, getting back in bed too. "I called and texted you a million times. We didn't want to leave without you but the last train was at two a.m."

My eyes were already closed. "Tell you about it later," I mumbled, before drifting away into sleep.

6

Put on a Happy Face

We all finally woke up around noon, and I ended up giving Max and Courtney the abbreviated version of the evening's events: cute guy, spent the night at his place, didn't really remember much else.

"I bet it was amazing," Max said dreamily.

"Yeah, he really did seem totally into you, Lu," Courtney said, a touch of envy in her voice.

Their heads were bobbing with romantic ideals of love-at-first-sight and tender kisses and feather beds. I drowned in embarrassment.

"I have to go home," I said abruptly, unable to keep talking about this.

I drove home in my pajamas.

Dad met me outside before I could even get out of my car. "I'm glad you're home, Lu. Are you ready to talk?"

"Is Lisa still here?"

"Yes," he said. "But I think once you talk to her—"

"I can't deal with this right now, Dad," I said, walking past him toward the house.

He didn't follow me. "Well, whenever you're ready, you know where to find us."

I ran straight upstairs to the bathroom—keeping my line of vision locked away from the living room and kitchen in case Lisa was there—and stood under the shower until the water ran cold, scrubbing my skin raw, rinsing, and scrubbing again, watching the remnants of last night cascade down the drain.

I spent the rest of the weekend in my room—homework, line memorizing, and guitar practice kept my attention, for the most part, away from the bad places.

Sunday night, Papa knocked on my door. "Lucy?" he called softly.

"Just leave it outside," I said, assuming he was there to deliver my dinner.

"Lucy, can I come in please?"

I strummed the guitar strings absentmindedly, debating.

"Come in," I said finally, only because it was him.

"Max called for you. He said he tried your cell but it was off. I told him you'd call him back later."

My phone's battery must have been dead. I hadn't taken it out of my bag to charge it all weekend. "Okay, thanks," I said.

Papa closed the door behind him and leaned against my bookshelf. "How you doing?"

I shrugged.

"Yeah," he said. "Me too."

There was a long stretch of silence.

"So that's it?" I said finally, my voice painted with bitterness. "She's here to stay? What happened to let's-all-share-our-feelings-and-sing-'Kumbaya'-and-decide-together?"

"Lucy, you ran away. You made it pretty clear that you didn't want to be involved in the discussion."

"So I freak out one time and now I just have to live with the consequences?"

Papa sighed. "Of course not. If you really don't want her here, then she's gone. But I do think…if you just spoke to her, it might help you understand *why* she's here. Maybe it will help you feel better about the whole thing."

I didn't say anything.

"Or maybe it won't," he said. "But I think it's worth a try. You can't spend the rest of your life in your room."

After Papa left, I rummaged through my bag in search of my phone. But as I did so, my fingers grazed something else in the bag—condoms. They were leftover from my Ty days, and I'd forgotten they were even in there. But they triggered something in the back of my mind. There were still two of them, intact and sealed in their wrappers.

I frantically thought back to Lee's cluttered apartment. There had been dust bunnies, dirty laundry, and a trashcan overflowing with empty soda bottles and crumpled up pieces of paper—but had I seen any condom wrappers? I couldn't remember.

I shook my head to clear my thoughts. Just because I didn't

remember seeing any wrappers didn't mean they weren't there. I'd just been in such a rush to get out of that apartment that I hadn't noticed them. Lee must've provided the condoms, which was why I still had these in my bag. Yes, that made sense. Even though I had been on the pill for over a year, I *never* had unprotected sex. Never, ever, ever.

But, Lucy, a little voice in my head whispered. *You never go out in the city or get drunk or have sex with guys you don't know, either.*

Shut up, I told the voice. I knew myself. And I knew that this was one rule I wouldn't have broken.

• • •

Sunday night, sleep was out of the question.

Lisa.

Lee.

Ty.

Elyse.

What I did Friday night—that wasn't me. I'd gone so far in my longing to escape from my life of late that I'd turned into someone else completely. And it just made me feel even worse.

I couldn't keep going on like this.

I needed to be me again.

There was a song from *Rent* about the importance of forgetting the past and living for today. I repeated the lyrics in my head like a mantra. Forget regret. Yes. Excellent advice.

The only question was, how?

• • •

I heard somewhere that just the physical act of smiling can actually make you happier. So Monday morning, I slapped on a smile and went downstairs for breakfast, determined to put the events of the weekend firmly behind me. I hugged my dads and uttered a polite "good morning" to Lisa, who was sitting in the chair that no one ever used.

"Good morning," she responded, surprised.

I coated an English muffin with grape jelly and settled down with yesterday's *New York Times Magazine*. But my attention kept drifting across the table. I hadn't had a chance to really look at Lisa until now. Her hair was short, sticking out from her head in inch-long spikes, and she was wearing deep red lipstick that was either skanky or sophisticated—I couldn't decide. Her face was fuller than I'd remembered, but there were new creases around her eyes.

Breakfast slunk by in itchiness. It was like it was our first day being filmed for a reality show: the cameras were on us and we knew we were supposed to act normal…but we had completely forgotten what normal was. No one said much of anything, and there were a lot of uncertain glances being darted around. Every clink of silverware against a plate or rustle of a newspaper seemed amplified in the otherwise silent atmosphere. But we got through it.

The week forged ahead, and gradually things started to make sense again. I continued to avoid Lisa, and she avoided me right back. I aced my pre-calculus test and I was the only one who handed in the extra-credit assignment in Honors English. Courtney and Max and I went shoe shopping at the mall. Rehearsals with Ty and Elyse were still uncomfortable, but I was getting better at ignoring them.

I even felt like the smiling thing was working. The more I smiled, the happier I felt. As the days went by, I didn't have to remind myself to smile at all.

7

Something Wonderful

A week after the Lee encounter, Andre finally dedicated an entire rehearsal to act 1, scene 4. Up until now, the schedule had been geared around Romeo and Juliet's scenes, with the supporting characters only getting partial rehearsal time. But Mercutio was undoubtedly the star of this scene, and I was eager to sink my teeth into it. I got to take center stage and give a long, crazy speech about Queen Mab, the fairy who puts dreams in our sleeping heads.

The scene also features Romeo, and it was oddly therapeutic to drop my inhibitions and dance around shouting nonsense right in Ty's face.

> *True, I talk of dreams;*
> *Which are the children of an idle brain,*
> *Begot of nothing but vain fantasy;*
> *Which is as thin of substance as the air,*
> *And more inconstant than the wind, who woos*

Even now the frozen bosom of the North,
And, being angered, puffs away from thence,
Turning his face to the dew-dropping South.

It was the end of a rather exhausting, exhilarating rehearsal, and I finished the speech for the final time that day, surprised when applause came from the dark house. I hadn't even realized people were watching. Shouldn't they have been getting measured for costumes or helping the tech crew paint flats or rehearsing their own scenes in the practice rooms? The house lights came up, and it turned out that the majority of the cast was there. I had no idea how long they'd been watching.

Andre came up onto the stage. "Excellent work today, everyone. Truly great job, Lucy." He squeezed my shoulder.

I couldn't help glancing at Elyse out in the audience. Did I detect a hint of jealousy in her gloomy expression?

Andre kept me a few minutes after to give me some notes, so most of my castmates were already gone by the time I packed up my things and left the auditorium.

I was surprised to find Evan waiting for me in the deserted hallway.

"Hey," I said.

He grinned and gave me a fist bump. "You killed it up there today," he said as we walked to the parking lot.

"Thanks. I had no idea everyone was watching."

"We weren't at first, but how could we not be lured in by a

beautiful girl shouting about giant cups of liquor and an old hag giving sex dreams to virgins? It was rad."

Beautiful girl? A deep blush warmed my cheeks.

"So, Lucy, you're single now, right?" Evan asked casually.

"Um, yeah."

He nodded. "Would you go out with me this weekend?"

"Go out?" I'd never been asked out on an actual date before. Ty and I had just sort of fallen together, growing closer as we spent time together at rehearsals and cast parties. There hadn't been much of an official courtship period.

"Yeah, you know, like I pick you up at your house and we go eat food together and maybe see a movie or something?"

I'd never really thought about Evan that way, but maybe this could be good. "Sure," I said. "Why not?"

• • •

Saturday night, he showed up at my doorstep at exactly seven o'clock. He looked different somehow. Maybe it was the absence of his baseball cap or the fact that he was wearing a gray button-down shirt that I'd never seen before. Or maybe it was that I was looking at him differently now. He was no longer just Evan, the new guy who had an encyclopedic knowledge about sword fighting. Now he was Evan, the guy who liked me, with whom I was about to spend the evening alone.

"You look really nice," he said.

"Thank you," I said, glad Max had convinced me to wear a dress.

"Want to meet my parents?" He didn't have much of a choice, since my dads were standing right behind me, dorky grins on their faces. Luckily, Lisa seemed to be lying low tonight—I wondered if my dads had asked her to stay in her room or if she did it on her own.

Evan's smile melted to surprise for the smallest fragment of a second as he added up the me + father + father equation, but he pulled it together a lot quicker than most people did, and the friendly smile returned to his face.

I introduced him to Dad and Papa, they all shook hands, my dads made the generic "treat our daughter well" remarks, and we were on our way.

"You have two dads," Evan said as we drove down the street.

"Indeed I do," I agreed.

"What's that like?" he asked.

I had to admire his brazenness. My town was pretty liberal as suburbs go, and my family had always been welcomed and accepted in Eleanor Falls, but people rarely asked direct gay-parent-related questions. They either overcompensated and acted like two men raising a teenage daughter was as commonplace as blue jeans and whitening toothpaste, though we always knew it was all they were thinking about, or they waited until they got to know us well before building up the courage to ask about it. But Evan had learned of my unconventional family all of two minutes ago and already he was asking questions. It was refreshing.

"It's all I've ever known," I said, shrugging. "It's normal to me."

"Are you adopted?" he asked.

I shook my head. "Not totally. I was half-adopted."

By the time I finished explaining the whole bio-dad/adopted-dad thing, we were at the restaurant.

After we ordered, Evan picked the conversation right back up and asked the question that no one had ever asked me outright before. "Have you ever met your biological mother?" It caught me off guard.

I took a sip of my soda, to give myself an extra moment to think. Could I justify telling Evan about Lisa being back, when I hadn't even told Courtney and Max? Maybe not, but I knew I was going to tell him anyway. There was something open about him.

"I have," I said. "Actually, she's staying with us right now."

"Oh, so you have a relationship with her then."

"Not exactly," I said, and dove into the whole sordid Lisa history. "She's been back a week now, and I still don't know why she's here. We've been doing a pretty good job of steering clear of each other."

He looked confused. "Why don't you just ask her?"

I let out a little laugh. "You make it sound so simple."

"Well, isn't it? You talk to her for two minutes, get her side of the story, and then decide whether she's worth your time or not. But by spending all your energy avoiding her and wondering why she's here, you're not being fair to yourself." He shrugged and took a bite of his mashed potatoes.

I stared at him in awe. "Who *are* you?"

"You mean, 'who is this random guy who thinks he knows anything about my life?'"

"I mean, 'who is this person who sees things so clearly?' I *wish* I could do that. I'm always overanalyzing everything—it's why I can't ever sleep. My mind won't shut up."

"Yeah, I'm the total opposite. I've never been a worrier. But that's not necessarily a good thing—things appear so cut-and-dried to me that I always think I'm right, which of course isn't true, and I end up putting my foot in my mouth." He paused. "You know, if we ever had kids, I bet they'd end up with a perfect mix of our two personality extremes."

I laughed. "Oh, so now we're having kids together, huh?"

He grinned. "Well, I think we kind of have to. Far be it from us to deny the world perfectly tempered, Shakespeare-quoting, Elizabethan fencing experts with your smile."

After dinner, we were having such a good time that we decided to forgo the movie and instead just drive around and talk. Evan told me all about his life back in San Francisco and how after his parents' divorce they didn't give him a choice of whether he wanted to stay in California with his dad or move here with his mom for her new job. He told me how he joined the drama club with a few guy friends freshman year because they'd heard it was a good place to meet girls and how, by the end of the first semester, his friends had all bailed but he had unexpectedly fallen in love with theater. We talked about Ty, and we talked about Sarah, Evan's ex-girlfriend.

"What happened with the two of you?"

"She left for college in Seattle, I came here, and that was the end of that." He gave a quick, unaffected shrug. I couldn't help feeling there was more to the story.

"Did you love her?"

He stared straight ahead. "I thought I did."

I sighed. I knew what that was like.

We sat there quietly for a while, parked on a side street a few blocks away from my house, listening to the radio. It wasn't an awkward lapse in conversation, though; it was comfortable. And after a few songs, Evan leaned over out of the blue and kissed me. It was soft and hesitant at first, but slowly grew deep and intense.

It was strange kissing someone other than Ty. Lee didn't count, because I didn't remember it. But Ty…I still remembered every kiss with him, from the very first to the very last. I remembered the softness of his lips and the way our teeth sometimes scraped against each other's and how we would laugh and go right on kissing. I remembered kissing him and thinking I never wanted to kiss anyone else for the rest of my life.

Kissing Evan was different. Not bad different, just…new. I liked the way he threaded his hands through my hair and I liked the way he seemed to be exploring my kiss rather than forcing his own on me. Reacting rather than acting.

We did a pretty good job of steaming up the car windows, but

Evan didn't try anything else. That was good—tonight made me excited for my future, but I still hadn't fully recovered from my past.

• • •

When I floated home from my date, the house was quiet. My dads had already gone up to bed, though their bedroom light was still on—I knew they were expecting me to check in with them before I went to bed. They were probably waiting to hear all about my night. The only light downstairs was coming from the living room. I went in to turn it off before I headed upstairs, but Lisa was sitting on the couch, using Dad's laptop.

"Oh. Sorry," I said. "I didn't know anyone was in here."

"It's okay," she said, closing the computer.

I gave a stiff nod and started to leave the room. But Evan's advice echoed in my ears. Lisa didn't deserve the effort it took to constantly avoid her. Papa did say he would kick her out if I asked him to. Maybe by this time tomorrow, she would be out of my life.

I slowly turned back around and sat in the chair opposite her.

"All right," I said. "You have two minutes to say whatever you want to say. Make it count."

8

Children Will Listen

Lisa took a deep breath. "I know you don't want me here," she said. "I guess I can't blame you. I don't really want to be here, either."

So far she wasn't making a very good case for herself. But I didn't say anything.

"Adam and Seth didn't tell you why I'm here, did they." It was more of a statement than a question.

I shook my head.

"I'm pregnant, Lucy."

My eyes instinctively darted to her stomach. She didn't *look* pregnant.

"Four months," she said, patting her midsection.

I cleared my throat. "Um, congratulations," I said. "But I still don't get what this has to do with us."

"I came here because, believe it or not, you and Adam and Seth are the only stable people in my life. And I need your help."

"With what? None of us have experience being pregnant."

"No. But when I was carrying you, Adam helped me...stay healthy."

That's when it all clicked. She needed us to help her stay away from *drugs*. I should have known it would be something like this. It was classic Lisa: irresponsible, selfish, and expecting everyone else to drop their lives in order to cater to her needs. She was the one with the drug habit, she was the one who went and got knocked up, and *we* were the ones who were supposed to deal with the consequences?

"I've been pregnant before," she continued. "I mean, besides with you. A few times, actually. But it never stuck…for one reason or another." She shrugged. "This time, though, I want to do it right."

Translation: *You were never good enough for me, but this baby is.* I felt like I'd been sucker-punched right in the center of my heart.

I pushed my chair back and stood up. "Your two minutes are up," I said, and went upstairs to bed.

• • •

The next morning I awoke to a knock at my door.

"Lucy?" Dad said. "Are you awake?"

"No!" I yelled, pulling the covers up over my head. I felt like I'd only just fallen asleep.

The door opened anyway, and Dad and Papa came in and sat on the edge of my bed.

"So, you spoke to Lisa," Dad said.

"And?" I mumbled.

"She said that she told you about the pregnancy."

I exhaled and pushed the covers back from my face. "You mean the pregnancy that for some reason we're expected to be responsible for, since she obviously has no self-control?"

Dad and Papa exchanged a look.

"Lucy," Papa said. "I meant what I said—if you really want her gone, she's gone."

"Okay, great. I want her gone."

"But hang on. Just think for a second about what that would mean."

"What?"

"She's already decided she's going to keep the baby. So if we kicked her out and she relapsed, that baby's health would be on our hands," Papa said. "Whether we like it or not, we're part of this now."

That was true…

"And remember," Dad said, "the baby is going to be your half-sibling."

Huh. That was also true.

"So you see the predicament we've been dealing with," Papa said.

"Yeah," I said after a moment. "I guess I do."

I was going to have a little brother or sister. Well, that just changed everything.

9
Memory

My feelings toward Lisa were so confusing—I hated her now more than ever, yet there was a lot less tension around the house now that we were all in agreement that she would stay with us at least until the baby was born.

I finally told Max and Courtney the whole story after rehearsal on Monday.

"So *that* explains why you've been acting so weird lately," Max said.

Well, partially.

"But why didn't you tell us?" Courtney asked.

"I'm really sorry," I said. "I guess I just had to work through it myself before I could talk about it with anyone."

Courtney gave me a big hug. "You can always come to us, Lucy."

I smiled gratefully. "Thanks, guys."

"Now let's get to the good stuff," Max said. "What's going on with you and Evan?"

"We've only been on one date, Max. It's way too early to tell." But I couldn't stop blushing.

That very morning, I'd left for school to find Evan waiting for me in the driveway, leaning against his car.

"Oh! Hi!" I said, surprised but not at all disappointed to see him.

"Hey," he said, and the corner of his mouth turned up.

We stood there like that for an extended moment, grinning at each other in the dewy morning air, and then sprang into action at the same time, our lips meeting before any other part of our bodies. I really hoped my dads weren't witnessing this, but it felt so good to be near Evan again that I didn't bother turning away from him to check.

When we finally did break apart, I played with the collar of his jacket and murmured, "So…what are you doing here? Not that I'm complaining."

"I woke up this morning with this grand plan to bring you breakfast and drive you to school," he said. "But it wasn't until I was pulling into your driveway that it dawned on me that you might think this was totally creepy and stalkery of me, showing up like this without calling. I don't want you to think I'm one of those possessive, no-woman-of-mine-is-gonna-drive-herself-places types."

"I don't think that," I said, laughing.

"Well, even so, I'm not driving you," he said decisively. "We'll take separate cars and meet at school."

"Evan, that's ridiculous. Not to mention bad for the environment."

He thought for a moment. "Okay, then you drive me to school."

He was so adorable. "Deal." He moved to get in the passenger side of my car. "Wait," I said. "What about breakfast?"

"Oh yeah!" He leaned in through his car window and took out several bags from various restaurants. "I didn't know what you liked, so I got a few choices." He spread everything out on the car hood. "OJ, coffee with milk and sugar, black coffee, and a good old-fashioned Coca-Cola in case you're pro-caffeine but anti-coffee."

I selected the black coffee with a wordless smile.

He nodded approvingly. "I like your style. And for food, we have a fine selection of bagel with cream cheese, fruit salad, jelly donut, and egg whites on whole wheat."

I chose the bagel and gave him a kiss on a cheek. "This was really sweet, Evan. Thank you."

He smiled. "You're welcome. Now, drive me to school, woman!"

I burst out in laughter.

• • •

We were growing closer. We started sitting together in homeroom and at lunch, and walking together hand-in-hand in the halls. He neglected the PSP in favor of hanging out with me and my friends during rehearsal downtimes. He made everything better. He knew nearly everything about me, and when my own mind twisted my feelings into an unmanageable ball of confusion, he had a way of making things clear and unintimidating. In some ways, after only a few weeks, Evan knew me better than Ty ever had. I had never even told Ty about Lisa. And he had never asked.

Ty and Elyse were now officially "an item," as my dads would call it. They'd taken their public displays of affection to a level only two drama queens could. They were *always* kissing and touching and rubbing each other. But like magic, the closer Evan and I became, the less I cared about Ty and Elyse. Several times I caught her darting a glance my way during a particularly touchy-feely moment between her and Ty, and it killed her that I wasn't fazed by it anymore.

One Friday night, as Evan and I were leaving the movies, he turned to me and said, "So are you my girlfriend now?" in that ultra-casual way of his.

I laughed. "That depends. Do you want me to be?"

"Oh definitely."

I grinned. "Well then, yes, I think I am."

"Cool," he said.

. . .

We'd been together nearly a month. Evan was over at my house, and for once Dad, Papa, and Lisa were all out. We were alone, up in my room, the door closed. I was playing him some songs on the guitar. But halfway through the second song, something happened. We locked eyes, my fingers stopped moving, the guitar was pushed to the side, and within two seconds we were all over each other.

We'd talked about sex before, but only in the context of our exes. Neither of us was a virgin. But we'd never talked about if or when we'd do it together. And now, it was looking like it was about to happen.

When Ty and I did it for the first time, it was a major production. We'd talked about it for months before we actually did it and planned out everything. The place, the day, the time, the music. Like everything in my life, I'd wanted it to be perfect.

It wasn't how I'd imagined. I felt weird, being completely naked in front of a boy, even a boy as beautiful and attentive as Ty. And the actual "doing it" part was so awkward. How should we position our bodies? What should we do with our hands? Where should we look? Should we be talking during it or just letting the moment speak for itself?

And it hurt. A lot. So much, in fact, that I still could not believe evolution hadn't figured out a solution to the whole hymen issue by now. It was over pretty quickly, and I was left wondering why everyone made such a *big deal* about sex.

Over time, though, I started to understand.

Just like I was understanding now. What it was like to want someone so badly, to feel that magnetic pull toward them, to think it impossible that your bodies could ever be close enough.

Evan's hands were in my hair, pulling me toward him as we kissed. My hands were on his chest, unbuttoning his shirt. I pushed the shirt back off his shoulders, and we parted, gasping, for the briefest of moments while we each yanked our t-shirts over our heads. Then we were back to kissing, and running our hands all over each other's bodies.

He was shirtless, I was in a bra, and we toppled over onto the bed together.

But as he moved to unbutton my jeans, I froze. Out of nowhere,

I was flashing back to the last time someone had undone my jeans—Lee. Memories from that night—drunken, lost memories that I thought I'd never see again—were charging back to me.

Stumbling down Spring Street to an apartment building with a red door.

Lee's callused guitar-player hands.

His stubble leaving red marks on my skin.

The tequila/cigarette mixture on his breath.

The sound my boots made as I yanked them off and dropped them to the floor.

Having sex several times throughout the night. Not once with protection.

Wait…what?

As that last image blazed across my memory, my entire body tensed up, and I stopped responding to Evan. Evan reacted to the change immediately and pulled back.

"Are you okay?" he asked, worried.

I nodded, my eyes squeezed shut. But I wasn't okay, not really.

"Did I do something wrong?"

I shook my head no. "It's not you," I whispered.

"Lucy, it's okay if you're not ready."

I took a few deep breaths, completely failed in my attempt to force Lee out of my brain, and sat up. "I'm sorry," I said. "I can't."

He studied me. I had no idea what he saw. "That's cool," he said finally, handing me my shirt.

I hadn't told Evan about the Lee night. It was probably the only thing I hadn't told him about myself, but I didn't want him to think I was the type of person who did things like that. So I didn't explain anything further now. And for the first time since I'd known him, he didn't ask any questions.

"You should go," was the last thing I said to him that night.

10
Consider Yourself

How had this *happened*?

I'd had unprotected sex. With someone I didn't even know. The thought was incomprehensible.

I felt like I'd let the whole world down. Ever since I was old enough to know about this stuff, the importance of safe sex had been drilled into my brain. Health teachers with their condom demonstrations, reality shows about teen pregnancy, television commercials for herpes medications, billboard advertisements for Planned Parenthood…and my dads. You'd think they were paid spokesmen for Trojan. At first, their casual tossing around of words like "prophylactic" and "spermicidal lube" embarrassed the hell out of me, but after a few years their open-forum approach to these topics became just another reason our relationship was so close.

Here's how the big "responsibility" talk went last year:

Dad: So, Lu, you and Ty seem to be getting serious.

Me: Yeah, I guess.

Papa: He's a cutie.

Me: I know, right?

Dad: (hands me a paper bag)

Me: (after peeking inside and finding the jumbo box of condoms) *Daaaad!*

Dad: It's important to be safe, sweetie; we can't stress that enough. Remember, no glove, no love.

Papa: There's also a drugstore gift card in there with a hundred dollars on it for when you need to stock up again.

Me: (my face still blazing with embarrassment) You know, none of my friends talk to their parents about stuff like this.

Dad: Well, none of your friends have parents that lived through the New York gay club scene in the nineties.

End scene.

I sat at my desk, twisting and untwisting a lock of my hair around my finger, weighing the potential consequences of my stupidity.

Pregnancy? No. I was on the pill, and I got my period right on time a few days after *the night*.

Sexually transmitted infections? I didn't really think that was much of a possibility, either. Lee and I had just been together that one time, and it didn't burn when I peed or anything. But on the other hand, I knew myself, and I knew my mind would be never be fully at ease—not to mention that I would never be able to move forward with Evan—unless I found out for sure. And this, at least, was something I was going to do right. So I did a ton of research.

Let me tell you something: the photos of various STIs on medical websites are not pretty. Those images alone are enough to make you declare condoms your best friend for life.

My first instinct was to go to my regular gynecologist to get tested. But then I realized that the tests would be on my insurance record and my dads would find out. Not that they'd be against my getting tested, but they'd definitely have questions as to why I thought it was necessary. And that was one conversation I did not want to have.

So I was going to go to a free health clinic in the city. I found one that actually specialized in STI testing, and you didn't even have to give your name. I could get this whole damn thing over with, and no one would ever need to know. Perfect.

I left for school in the morning like I always did, but instead of turning into the school parking lot, I kept driving south, straight toward Manhattan. I parked in a garage and walked to the Harlem address that I'd scrawled on a Post-It. It was a random, nondescript three-floor building with no signs or anything indicating I was in the right place. The doctors' offices I was used to were in shiny, large office buildings, with security desks and potted plants. This place didn't feel at all welcoming, but I forced myself to push on. I was here for a reason. I pressed the buzzer for the lower level and was buzzed in a few seconds later. I took the elevator one flight down to the windowless basement and had to be buzzed in through a second door.

"Good morning," the man at the front desk greeted me.

"Hi," I replied quietly.

"How may I help you?" he asked.

Didn't he know? Didn't everyone come here for the same reason? I just stared at him, not wanting to say it out loud.

He smiled curiously back at me. "Are you here for one of our group meetings? Or for our needle exchange?"

I shook my head. "You do STI screenings here, right?" I finally asked. I felt weird saying it out loud.

"Oh, yes, of course," the man said, and handed me a pen. "Please sign in—first name and last initial. Someone will be with you shortly."

I wrote "Lucy M." and my arrival time on the sheet taped to the desk, and sat down in the waiting room.

Almost every seat was taken; the room was packed with people. Mostly men. The walls were painted red—I guess in an effort to make the place seem less depressing—and there were posters pinned up everywhere, with sayings like, "Think you picked up more than you bargained for at that party last night?" and "BYOC: Bring Your Own Condom."

One by one, like a graduation procession, people were called from the waiting room. I waited and tried not to stare at anyone. My leg shook uncontrollably, and the man sitting next to me had to ask me to stop. I apologized and saw the curiosity in his eyes as he caught a glimpse of my face. He was probably wondering what a girl like me was doing here. I was wondering the same thing.

Time crept by. I tried to read through my script, but it was like my eyes and my brain had been disconnected. *Wisely and slow. They stumble that run fast.* I read the same line over and over again, registering no meaning. It was three hours before they called my name.

I followed a middle-aged woman into an "interview room." She was wearing white pants and a white jacket, but she introduced herself as simply "Marie" and was wearing a whole lot of tacky gold jewelry, so I was pretty sure she wasn't a doctor. The room was stocked with medical supplies, and there were more posters on the wall. "Syphilis is Back!" one shouted at me. Marie indicated that I should sit in the chair across the table from her.

"So, Lucy," she began, with a cheerful smile. "What brings you here today?"

"Um, I wanted to get tested for STIs," I said. Why did they keep making me say it?

Marie nodded. "What do you think the likelihood of a positive result is for you today?"

"Pretty low. But I just want to be sure."

"That's very smart of you. All right, let's get started. I'm going to ask you several questions. You'll see me writing your answers down, but it's just for our records—anything you tell me will be kept confidential, so please be as accurate and honest as you can."

I nodded.

"First, I am legally required to ask you what you will do if you test positive for HIV today," she said, pen poised.

I blinked. "What do you mean?"

"If you test positive, how do you think you will react?" she rephrased.

What kind of a question was that? How would anyone know how they would react until actually put in that situation? That was like asking what you would do if you woke up to find your house was on fire. Would you run out immediately? Stop to call 911? Look for your cat? Put on your shoes? Dash around collecting valuables? Until you're actually in that burning building, flames scorching your skin, there's no way to know for sure.

"I don't know," I answered truthfully.

"I need something to put down here. Just take your best guess," Marie said with a flippant hand gesture, as if she were fully aware of the ridiculousness of the question.

"I, uh, guess I would try to work through it as best I could," I said.

"Okay, that's fine," she said, scribbling on her form. "We just have to ask that because some people say they will try to hurt themselves or someone else, and we'd have to report that. All right, next question. How many sexual partners have you had in the last year?"

"Two."

"Have you had sex for money, drugs, or clothing?"

What the…? "No."

"Have you had sex with a man who also has sex with men?"

Whoa. I had no idea the questions were going to be so personal. I wasn't feeling anything close to comfortable, in this strange room in this strange building answering this strange woman's strange questions, but still I answered. "Not that I know of."

"Have you ever been sexually assaulted?"

And so the questions continued. I felt my cheeks burning deeper red with each mention of words like "oral," "vaginal," "anal," and "group sex."

The interview went on for over twenty minutes. Most of the questions, about things like drug use and pregnancy, I could answer no to immediately. But some of the questions hit closer to home.

"Have you had unprotected sex in the last year?"

"Have you had sex under the influence of alcohol?"

"Have you had sex with someone who wasn't your regular partner?"

"Have you had sex with an anonymous partner?"

"Have you had sex with an IV drug user?"

The more times I responded yes, the more unnerved I became. They don't ask these questions for fun. They ask them because they are relevant to the contraction of STIs. I began to realize that every time I answered yes, my chance of actually having contracted something increased. By the end of the interview, I was freaking out.

Marie had me sit in a different chair, where I rested my arm on a padded table-like attachment. Without much of a warning, she stuck me with a needle and drew three vials of blood: "One for your syphilis test and one for hepatitis C. And one for your HIV confirmatory test, if necessary," she explained. "And now for the chlamydia and gonorrhea sample." She handed me a little cup and directed me to the bathrooms across the office. "Fill this, seal it up, and bring it back here when you're finished."

If there's anything more embarrassing than peeing in a cup, it's having to walk all the way back across the clinic office, past workers' cubicles, holding said cup of pee. Several clinic employees looked up from their computer screens as I passed. Some gave me a patronizing smile. Most looked hurriedly away the moment they saw what I was carrying. I told myself that they see this all the time, that they aren't bothered by the sight of a little urine. But that didn't make me any less humiliated.

After handing off the cup to Marie, she handed me a little plastic stick with a swab-like tip. It looked like a pregnancy test. I looked at her, confused.

"This is for the HIV rapid test," she told me. "Smile like you're brushing your teeth, and swab your outer gums, once across the top and once across the bottom."

I did as she said and handed the stick back to her. She placed it in a little machine, and told me the HIV results would be ready in thirty minutes. I'd have to call the office in ten days for the other test results.

It was officially the longest half-hour of my life. Stuck in this smaller, blander waiting room specially designated for people waiting on their HIV test results, shifting restlessly in my orange plastic chair, unable to concentrate on anything except the other people in the room and the clock.

In the far corner, a frazzled woman in a bad wig was trying to keep her two rugrats occupied. A few chairs over from her was a couple who looked like they frequented the free clinic—the rings of black makeup smudged under her eyes hinted that she hadn't washed her face in at least a week, and they both had track marks up their arms. They were draped over each other like they were each other's life force. Over in the far corner was the oldest person in the room by a mile. He had wispy white tufts of hair on his head, he was wearing enormous eyeglasses that he'd probably had since about 1982, and his hands were wrinkled and worn. Definitely not the type of person I would have expected to see in a place like this. And next to me, a skinny pale guy who looked only a couple of years older than I was slouched low in his chair, his arms crossed over his chest, the hood of his purple hoodie pulled down over his eyes. His breathing was rhythmic. Was he actually *sleeping*?

I stuffed my iPod earbuds in my ears. I needed a distraction. The music filled my head, and I began to stage a full-on production of *A Chorus Line* in my head. It was something I did on long train rides or when my chronic insomnia was holding me prisoner at night. But the moment the opening song's lyrics kicked in, I suddenly couldn't turn it off fast enough. The song was called "I Hope I Get It," of all things. Yeah, not exactly the sentiment I needed in my head right now.

I switched to the more tone-appropriate *Les Misérables* and glanced up at the numbers on the display for the tenth time in the last minute. They remained stubborn, torturing me, mocking me each time I met their stare. Still serving numbers sixty through sixty-four. I shot them a look of contempt and wrenched my eyes away again—only to realize with horror that the black ink on the slip of paper clutched in my hand had grown blurred and spidery in my sweaty palm. I frantically shook it out, striving to keep it legible. It wasn't much, but right now this tiny piece of paper held the only information in the world that mattered.

Name: Lucy M.
Age: 16
Number: 68

I smoothed it out and set it on my knee to dry. If I continued clutching onto it in my sweaty hands, it would soon be completely illegible, and Marie had warned me that I wouldn't be given my results without presenting the paper to the social worker. There was no way in hell I was going to go through all the waiting and questioning and testing again, just so I could get another ticket.

At long last, the digital sign changed. Now serving numbers sixty-five through sixty-eight.

My number was up.

11

This is the Moment

A clinic employee had us line up in a little hallway, in order by number. First in line was the old man, followed by the young guy, the lady and her kids, and me.

A frizzy-haired woman in an out-of-style business suit came out of an office and called the first man inside. They were behind the closed door for less than three minutes, and then he left, relief inscribed across his face. The scene repeated with the young guy. As he left, he grabbed a handful of free condoms from a bin and stuffed them in his pockets. The woman was called in next.

"Could you watch them, please?'

It took me a minute to realize she was talking to me.

"Huh?" I said.

"Could you just keep an eye on my kids while I go in?"

I glanced at the two little boys. One was about four years old and running up and down the hallway, arms out like an airplane, and the other was about two and actively trying to bust out of his stroller. This was so not what I needed right now.

"Uh…" I said, frantically trying to come up with a reason why I couldn't watch this woman's kids, but my brain wasn't working right. "Okay, sure."

"Great," she said, and disappeared into the office.

As soon as they realized they'd been left alone with a stranger, the kids stopped their fidgeting and stared, wide-eyed, up at me.

"Um, hi," I said, trying to sound cheery. "I'm Lucy. What are your names?"

No answer.

"Uh…what's your favorite color?" I didn't have much experience with children. I'd never even been a babysitter.

"Where's my mom?" the older boy asked.

"Oh, she'll be right back. She's just talking to the lady in that room."

"Why?"

Umm.

"Because the lady has some information for her."

"Why?"

I sighed. "I don't know, kid."

"Are you waiting to talk to the lady too?"

"Yes."

"Why?"

How did I get myself into these situations?

"It's a long story."

"I like stories," he said.

"Well, this is a grown-up story."

He studied me. "Are *you* a grown-up?"

"I…"

Good question. I sure as hell didn't feel like one right now.

Finally, *finally*, the woman came out of the office and collected her children. She didn't even say thank you. I watched them leave.

"Number sixty-eight?"

I turned—the office lady was looking at me expectantly. I was the only one left.

I took a deep breath and followed her into the office.

"I'm Diane Sullivan, the clinic's social worker," she said, extending her hand. "It's nice to meet you"—she took my ticket and consulted her chart—"Lucy M."

I shook her hand and sat down.

As Diane flipped through my file, my heart was sprinting. I'd never believed in psychics or clairvoyance or that kind of thing, but my intuition was screaming at me right now. Somehow, I *knew* something was wrong. I could feel it.

Diane looked me in the eye. Her expression was smooth.

"Lucy, your rapid HIV test result is reactive," she said in a calm, neutral tone.

I stared at her. What did that mean? Didn't she know this was not the time for being cryptic? "Reactive?" I repeated.

"Yes. That means you have received a preliminary positive result."

Positive. That was a word I could understand.

An involuntary gurgle escaped my throat, and suddenly the

world was closing in on me, disappearing from the outside edges in. I thrust my head between my knees.

Positive.

I couldn't breathe.

Why can't I breathe? I asked the demons in the room. Their black, beady eyes were on me. I felt them. *Where's the air? What did you do?*

The demons didn't say anything. They just watched me. Judging. Planning.

Something touched my back. I jumped out of my skin. "Don't touch me!" I shrieked at the demons, spending the last of my air. "You're trying to kill me!"

But the voice that answered didn't make sense. It didn't match the demons' greedy, evil faces. "Lucy, breathe with me. In…out…"

How do they know my name?

But I obeyed. I had no choice.

"In…out…that's right…in…"

I gasped and choked. The oxygen that did manage to get in was soothing.

"Very good, Lucy. In…out…in…"

After a few minutes, I was able to sit upright again. I opened my eyes. The demons were gone. Or hiding.

Diane was back.

My natural breathing returned, and I didn't have to focus on getting air anymore. But I still felt sick to my stomach.

"Are you all right, Lucy?" Diane asked, calm as ever.

No. Of course I wasn't.

But I was coherent enough now to know that she was talking about my immediate state, not the bigger picture. I gave a tiny nod.

"Now, we have a lot to discuss." She flipped through my file again, taking her time to review the pages where Marie had written my answers down. "Given your established risk behaviors, it's crucial that you make some changes so you don't expose anyone else to the virus." She looked up at me. "And it's also very important for you to have a reliable support system to help you work through this confusing time. Have you thought about who you will discuss your result with?"

I stopped listening to Diane and her social worker dribble.

My risk behaviors, she said. I didn't *have* risk behaviors. I just made one stupid mistake. I didn't deserve this.

Suddenly, I couldn't sit in this room one second longer.

I pushed out of my chair and ran. Diane called after me, but I shut her out. I ran down the hall, through the waiting room, through door number one, up the stairs, through door number two, and into the real world. I didn't care that people were staring. I didn't care that I looked like hell. I just kept running.

I ran until my feet screamed. Then I slowed to a walk and glanced at a street sign. I'd gone over forty blocks. But I kept going.

I felt empty. It's the only way to describe it. I couldn't think, I couldn't cry. *Positive.* It was as if the word was some sort of incantation, and now that it had been uttered, a spell had been cast. Diane had sucked all the reason, hope, and life out of me, and all I'd been left with was a hollow shell of a body and a brain that wouldn't work.

So I walked.

There's something about New York City that gives you permission to just *be*. There's no need for pretense, no need for masks. You can be real, without risk. The buildings are your protectors, the streets are your tethers. The people…you will never see them again. Even when they're right in front of you, you don't see them. Not really. Just as they don't really see you. New York is beautifully anonymous.

As one wave of New Yorkers disappeared underground, another emerged. I took my time, watching them. Each one of them on their way somewhere, each with a purpose.

Except me. I was still empty.

The sun was low in the sky when my bag started vibrating. I ignored it.

I passed a homeless man. He was reading a thick book, and a dog was curled up on a blanket beside him. I gave him all my money. Fifty-six dollars and ninety-three cents.

"God bless you," he said.

It's a little late for that, the voice in my head responded.

Somehow, I made it back to the parking garage. Somehow, I got in my car and made it go. And somehow, I ended up back at home.

12
On My Own

"You're home early," Dad said cheerfully.

I was? It felt like years since I'd been home.

"Did rehearsal let out early today?"

Oh yeah. Rehearsal. That's where I should be right now if the world made sense.

He looked at me curiously. "Are you feeling okay?" He placed a hand on my forehead.

No. I'm not, Dad, I wanted to say.

"Answer me, Lucy. Are you sick?"

Ha. Am I sick? That's funny.

It took a while to for me to realize that I was actually laughing. Out loud. Hysterically. Manically.

Dad got on the phone. "Seth, are you on your way home yet? Something's wrong with Lucy…No, I don't know…She came home early and she's acting strangely and she's really pale…I don't know…Okay…Okay, bye."

Dad placed a glass of water in front of me. "Drink," he ordered.

I was still laughing. I didn't want to be. But I couldn't stop. I felt possessed. Dad physically put the glass in my hand and guided it to my mouth. "Drink," he said again.

I managed to gulp down a mouthful of the water. It was cold and I felt it travel down down down through my body.

My body. My poisoned, tainted body.

The lingering giggles transformed into huge, heaving sobs.

"Lucy, please talk to me. What's going on?" Dad pleaded.

I swallowed and, through chattering teeth, attempted speech. "I…I'm…" I began. But what was I going to say?

Positive. I couldn't say the word out loud.

"I…think I have the flu," I managed. "I need to go to bed."

"You must have a fever—you're delirious," Dad said. "I'm going to call the doctor, see if she can see you tonight."

I shook my head fiercely. "No, no doctor! I'll be fine." I booked it upstairs to my room before he could argue.

You are nothing but a stupid, spoiled child, I told myself over and over again.

I knew now that there was no one to blame but me. I'd made excuses for running off with Lee, blaming Lisa and Ty and Elyse for messing with my head, and messing with my life. But no one had forced me into his bed that night. This was *my* fault.

I'd had everything. And then a few things didn't go my way and I ran away and threw a tantrum like a two-year-old. Of course I was being punished. That's what happens to kids who act out.

. . .

I shut myself off from the world. Tuesday and Wednesday came and went without me ever seeing the sun. I didn't go to school; I didn't go to rehearsal; I didn't return Evan or Andre or Max or Courtney's barrage of calls. I didn't listen to music; I didn't put on the TV; I didn't do any schoolwork. I didn't shower. I barely ate.

I didn't sleep much, either; my head was teeming with answer-less questions:

Will I get AIDS?

Will I die?

Will my dads hate me?

Will my friends abandon me?

Will I ever be able to have sex again?

Will I ever be able to have a baby?

Will I ever be able to be on Broadway?

Will I have to go on medication?

Will anyone ever love me?

. . .

I don't know what day it was, maybe late Tuesday. But it was defi-nitely the middle of the night. The house was quiet and dark.

I got out of bed and flipped on every light in my room. Then I stripped off my pajamas and stood, naked and illuminated, in front of my full-length mirror. The person staring back was not me. She was a near-perfect copy, right down to the tiny mole on my left hip bone and the thin scar on my left hand that I never could remember getting.

But her skin was like tracing paper, and the light made her transparent.

And on the inside, she was all wrong.

• • •

Wednesday afternoon, Max and Courtney came by my house. It was quiet, and I was able to hear everything that was said downstairs.

"Hey, guys, come on in," Dad said.

"Is Lucy here? She's been MIA all week," Max said, sounding worried.

"And she hasn't been answering her phone," Courtney added.

"She's been home sick," Dad replied, and then lowered his voice an ineffective smidge. "Between us, though, I think there might be something else going on. Do either of you know if anything happened that would make her not want to go to school? Something with Ty or Evan, maybe?"

"I can't think of anything," Courtney said.

"Me either," said Max.

"Hang on—you said all week? She wasn't in school Monday?" Dad asked.

"Nope," Max said.

There was a moment where I couldn't hear anything. Maybe they were talking too low, or maybe they weren't talking at all. Dad must have been putting the pieces together that I hadn't been in school the day I came home all messed up. It didn't matter. What was he going to do, ground me?

"Can we see her?" Courtney asked.

There was a pause, and then Dad said, "Let me check and see if she's up for having company."

A few seconds later, there was a knock on my door and Dad came in. "Max and Court are here for you."

I rolled over in my bed so my back was to him. "No visitors," I mumbled.

"Honey, they're worried about you. It might make you feel better to see your friends."

"*No visitors*," I repeated, and covered my face with a pillow, shutting out the light.

Dad stood there for a moment and then left. I didn't bother listening to whatever excuse he gave my friends.

• • •

If I told my family and my friends the truth, everything would change. They would look at me differently, treat me differently. Of course they would—I *was* different. But right now I was the only one who knew it. And that was the safest place to be. Because if the world outside me became as unrecognizable as the world *inside* me had, I honestly wouldn't know what to do.

On the other hand, if no one knew, they would still be expecting me to be the same old Lucy. But how do you play the role of yourself when "yourself" no longer exists?

• • •

Because I adamantly refused to go see the doctor, my dads assumed there wasn't anything really wrong with me and made me go back to school after two days.

Thursday morning, I pulled into my usual parking spot to find Max waiting for me, leaning against his car, ankles and arms crossed. He didn't move as I turned off the engine and got out of the car. He just watched me, his eyes hidden behind his retro, mirrored sunglasses.

"Hey," I said lifelessly.

"Really? That's all you have to say?" he said.

"What do you mean?"

"I mean you *disappeared*, Luce. No calls, no texts, not even a Facebook status update to let the world know you were alive. The only reason I knew you were coming back today was because I talked to your dads. What the hell is going on with you?" he said.

"I was sick," I said.

"You were so sick that you couldn't even pick up the phone to let one of us know that you wouldn't be in rehearsal? Since when is that how you treat your friends? We were *worried* about you."

"I'm sorry, okay? It won't happen again."

Max sighed and dropped his arms. "Is this about Lisa being back?" His voice was a little softer now.

"No."

"So what's wrong?"

"Nothing is wrong, okay?" I began to walk toward the school's entrance. "Now let's go, we're gonna be late."

• • •

The moment we walked into the drama club homeroom, a hush fell over the room. Time stopped, and I stood there like an animal at the zoo. Like a freak on display.

They can see it, the voice in my head whispered. *They can see through your skin. They know.*

I had to get out of there.

In slow motion, I twirled back toward the door. All I had to do was get down the hall and out of the school and into my car and away from the prying eyes. Home schooling couldn't be that bad—

Then suddenly, as if on cue, everyone started talking at once. "Oh my god, how are you feeling?" "Where have you *been*?" "That wasn't cool, Lucy; you don't even have an understudy!"

Wait…maybe they *didn't* know.

"Some of us were pretty sure you were dead," Elyse said, not sounding particularly concerned.

My head scrambled to keep up. They were acting like this just because I was away for a few days? But that was so ridiculous! Kids stayed home sick and took mental health days all the time. Just because I'd gotten the perfect attendance award every year since eighth grade didn't mean I wasn't entitled to a break.

But they really couldn't tell. They didn't know. I was so relieved.

Courtney watched me from across the room. I couldn't read

her expression—it was something between scowling and questioning—but before I could go over and talk to her, I was sidetracked.

Ty appeared in front of me and spoke to me for the first time since we'd broken up. "Welcome back," he said. "Everyone really missed you."

"Not everyone," I said, nodding in Elyse's direction.

"Okay, *almost* everyone," he admitted with an apologetic grin. "I mean it, though—it hasn't been the same without you."

His dark eyes burned into mine, and for the smallest moment I wondered if maybe he was talking about more than just the play. But then a warm hand clasped around my wrist, and I was being pulled out into the hallway.

"Are you okay?" Evan whispered once we were alone.

I nodded weakly.

He took a deep breath. "So look…if you don't like me anymore, you can just tell me. I can handle it."

I blinked, uncomprehending.

"What are you talking about?" I asked.

"I'm talking about what happened last weekend in your room. Things ended weird that night, and then you fell off the face of the planet for nearly a week."

"Wait—you think I was avoiding you?" I couldn't help but laugh a little.

"Weren't you?" he said, less sure now.

"No, of course not."

"So what was it?"

"I was sick."

He waited for more of an explanation, but I was overwhelmed and trying to keep it together and that was the best I could do.

"So you…still like me?"

"I still like you," I said, and it was the truth.

But as soon as the words passed through my lips, I knew I should have lied.

13

It's a Hard-Knock Life

Here's the entirety of what I knew about HIV:

1. It's the virus that causes AIDS.

2. It's communicable through unprotected sex and needle sharing.

3. It's incurable.

It wasn't much; I needed to know more. So, one night that weekend, after everyone else had gone to bed, I went online. It only took a few quick keystrokes to discover that when it came to the subject of HIV and AIDS, the Internet was a bottomless well of overwhelmingly depressing statistics. But I just couldn't look away. As the data piled up, my outlook became increasingly pessimistic. But at least I was beginning to get answers to some of my questions.

I learned that, apart from sex and IV drug use, the two main routes of HIV contraction are breast milk and perinatal transmission—which means a mother passing it onto her baby. So, no, I would never be able to give birth to my own child.

I learned that, for most people, HIV progresses to AIDS within ten years. For some, it takes longer, and for some, it happens much sooner. So, yes, at some point, most likely before I turned thirty, I would get AIDS.

I learned that AIDS killed over twenty-five million people between 1981 and 2006, and several more million since then. So, yes, I was going to die. And not in the, "Oh, everyone dies someday, but only after they've lived an extra-long life and had kids and grandkids and great-grandkids" way. I was going to die in the far-too-young, oh-so-tragic way.

I pressed on and learned what, exactly, that death would look like. It was ironic—I'd sung along to the *Rent* song "Will I?" about a thousand times without ever really thinking about the meaning behind the words. But now, for the first time, I understood why the characters were asking if they would lose their dignity. It was because that's what AIDS does to its victims. There would be lesions and loss of bowel control and high fevers. But those are just super-fun bonuses of the syndrome—they wouldn't kill me. There was no knowing what would finally take me out in the end. AIDS makes your immune system basically useless, so that you're susceptible to all kinds of illnesses and unable to fight them off. So it could be cancer or liver disease or even pneumonia…but whatever it was, it was guaranteed to be undignified.

But as hard as these facts were hitting home, they were still just words. I needed to see it, in living color. So, in a morbid fit of self-sabotaging curiosity, I did an image search. In less than a second, my computer screen was filled with dozens of the most awful photographs I had ever seen. Horrifyingly thin, failing bodies hooked up to oxygen machines. Skin covered in lesions so bad it looked like it was rotting. The helpless, pleading faces of African children staring straight into my soul.

A shiver rolled over me, and I grabbed my trash can just in time for it to catch a surge of vomit. It was as if my body was trying to rid itself of what it had just seen. As if it was trying to evict the sickness that was taking up residence inside.

But I couldn't unsee what I'd seen—even when I closed my eyes the images were still there.

And I couldn't get rid of the virus. If there was anything my little Internet excursion had reinforced in my brain, it was that.

As quickly as I could manage, I erased my browsing history. Then I turned off my lights and dove under my covers and vowed never to allow myself to be tempted into researching this disease ever again.

14
What I Did For Love

Like always, my mind wouldn't shut up. When I heard that the flu was going around, I panicked, worrying about what would happen if I caught it. When I brushed my teeth a little too hard and spit out blood-tinted toothpaste, I questioned if I should douse the sink with bleach to kill any left-behind bacteria. During class, I tuned out the teacher and studied my classmates, wondering if anyone else was carrying around a secret like this.

The worst part was that I felt totally fine. Exactly the same as always. But I *wasn't* fine. My body was lying to me. It was deceiving me, and everyone I knew, into believing that it was healthy. And that made me hate it even more.

The thing they don't tell you in sex education classes is what to do *after*. It's all, "Don't do this, don't do that. And if you *do* do this or that, make sure you do it safely." But what about when you screw up? Then what? Where do you go? Who do you tell? How do you act? Sex "education" prepares you for nothing.

So, for lack of any better ideas, I went on autopilot: school, rehearsal, homework, chores. Keep up appearances on the outside, and no one would know what going on inside. But it was arduous work; the HIV that crept and crawled through my veins was all I could think about.

When my phone buzzed on the weekends or after school with calls from Max or Courtney, I sent them to voicemail. It was hard enough trying to act normal during the day. I could only pretend so much.

I was completely lost, but it actually looked like my act was working. At least, no one said anything that made me think otherwise.

No one except Evan, that is. He knew something was up. And I knew why. I may have managed to put up a passable façade everywhere else in my life, but there was no way I could fake intimacy. Every time he tried to hold my hand or move in for a kiss, I recoiled. I no longer knew how to be in a physical relationship. How could I share my body with someone when it felt alien to me?

"All right, Lucy," he said with a sigh as he drove me home after rehearsal. "Just say it."

I looked at him. "Just say what?"

"Whatever it is that's going on in that head of yours." His brown eyes were clear and his face was smooth. He wasn't angry. He should have been; I wouldn't have blamed him. But he seemed like all he was after was an explanation.

Of course, that was the other thing I couldn't give him.

Instead, the words I had been thinking all week but trying not to say flowed out of me before I could stop them. "I think we should break up," I whispered. I meant it too—he would be far better off without me.

Evan swallowed and nodded, but his expression didn't change much. I realized he'd been expecting me to say that.

"Why?" he asked.

I looked away. "I don't know."

"That's not good enough. Give me a real reason."

"It's...just not working. With us. You know?"

"But that's what I don't get," he said quietly. "It *was* working. You said you wanted to be my girlfriend. I don't understand what changed."

I opened my mouth to reply, but nothing came out.

"Lucy, I love—"

I sucked in my breath sharply. "Don't say that," I said, and ran out of the car and into my house, slamming the door behind me.

I threw myself onto my bed and buried my face in my pillows to muffle my sobs. It was the first time I'd cried since I broke down in front of my dad that first day. I felt like my heart was being shredded apart. The pain was so bad that it was almost...good. At least I was feeling *something*. It reminded me, albeit in a sick, terrible way, that I wasn't dead just yet.

But my meltdown was interrupted by a knock on the door.

God, why couldn't I just have parents who ignored me, like everyone else did?

"Come in," I croaked.

I was startled to find that it was Lisa. She hadn't set foot in this room since she'd blown back into town.

She handed me an envelope.

"What's this?"

"It's a picture of the baby. I went to the doctor today. My five-month checkup," she said.

I studied the ultrasound image. I didn't know what to think, sitting there holding tangible evidence that life goes on with or without you. So all I said was, "Is its head supposed to be that big?"

Lisa shrugged. "Yeah, they said that's normal. Yours must have looked like that too. I don't really remember."

I slid the photo back in its envelope and handed it back to her.

"It's a girl," she said.

I blinked. "Really?"

"Yeah." Lisa looked like she was expecting something more from me, but I didn't know what else I was supposed to say. "Aren't you going to congratulate me?" she asked eventually.

"Oh. Uh, yeah. Congratulations."

She beamed. "Thank you," she said, like she hadn't just had to pry that out of me.

"Do you know what you're going to name her?" I asked.

"Not yet. Maybe you could help me come up with something?"

What was this? Mother-daughter bonding time? "Oh. Um, I don't know. I'll…think about it."

"Okay," Lisa said. "Good."

15

The Past is Another Land

"I still don't get it," Max was saying. "Why did you break up with him, again?"

We were in the cafeteria. Evan hadn't arrived yet, so it was just me, Max, and Courtney, and Max was pelting questions at me like I was on trial.

"I *told* you, it just wasn't working," I said for the zillionth time.

"*What* wasn't working? He's hot and he adores you. This doesn't make any sense," he said, popping open his Diet Coke with an incensed flourish.

I turned to Courtney, who hadn't been saying much. "You understand, right, Court? When it's not right, it's just not right. Must be a women's intuition thing," I said with a little shrug, hoping getting her on my side would make Max feel outnumbered and give up on the whole subject.

But Courtney surprised me. She put her sandwich down and sat back in her chair. "You know what, Lucy? I *don't* understand. In case you haven't noticed, I've never even had a boyfriend. And neither has Max, unless you're counting online relationships."

Max stuck his tongue out at her. "There's nothing wrong with Internet dating."

"That's not the point. We're here, desperately wanting what you always seem to find so easily, and you don't even appreciate what you have when you have it. You broke up with Evan on no more than a whim, as far as I can tell, and now you want me to back you up on that? Gimme a break."

Max burst into a round of applause. "Amen, sister."

I glowered back at them, unmoved. They weren't going to make me feel bad.

I *did* have a good reason for breaking up with Evan. Courtney was accusing me of being selfish, when I was actually doing the most unselfish thing I knew to do.

"Whatever," I said, pushing away my untouched lunch.

"What the hell is going *on* with you, Luce?" Max demanded.

"I don't know what you're talking about."

"Oh really, you don't?" he said sarcastically. "Well, lemme fill you in. You're *obviously* lying to us about whatever it was that happened with Evan, and you've been acting really freaking weird since your little disappearing act last week."

They'd noticed? "No, I haven't!"

Max glared at me. "Okay, you're right, *weird* isn't the right word. *Bitchy* is more like it."

I felt like I'd been slapped across the face. I stared at Max. He stared right back, unblinking. I kept waiting for Courtney to say something, to stick up for me, to tell Max he was overreacting. But neither of them said anything, and his last words hung heavy over our table.

"You know what, Max?" I said finally. "You really don't under-stand anything, so just shut up." Then I pushed out of my chair and stormed out of the lunchroom.

I rounded the corner, blood boiling, intending on spending the rest of the lunch period in the auditorium, and of course, that's when I crashed right into Evan.

I dropped my bag, and books, pens, and makeup spilled everywhere.

"Oh. Sorry," he said, helping me collect everything.

"It's fine," I said automatically, silently cursing the fates.

"Where are you going?"

"To the auditorium. Why?"

"Well, I was hoping we could eat lunch together," he said.

I was so not in the mood for whatever this was. "Why?"

He handed me back my bag and squared his shoulders. "Because I decided to give you another chance."

I swore silently.

"You do remember our conversation yesterday afternoon, right?" I said.

"Yeah. But I don't accept."

"It's not your choice, Evan."

"But why not? Who says you get to decide whether we get to be together or not?"

"Um, life? The world? That's how these things work: if you don't want to be with someone anymore, you get to decide that. Relationships are not democracies." I hitched my bag further up onto my shoulder. "I have to go."

I turned to leave, but Evan caught my wrist. "Lucy."

"Let me go. Please, just…let me go." I wriggled out of his grasp and continued down the hall, not looking back.

• • •

It was the day from hell. And it wasn't over yet.

At least luck was on my side in one infinitesimal respect: we were working on act 2, scene 4 in rehearsal. That meant I didn't have to have any on-stage interaction with Evan, Max, or Courtney. It was just me, Ty, and our Nurse and Benvolio. (Amazing how being around Ty suddenly didn't seem that formidable compared with everything else.) But even so, the vibe of the whole rehearsal was horrible. Max and Courtney were obviously avoiding me. But what did they even have to be mad about? They weren't the ones who'd been accused of being a bitch. Evan, on the other hand, wouldn't leave me alone, even though he *should* have been the one avoiding me.

He was like a harpy, lingering around in the wings for any little break or moment where he could swoop in and try to get my attention. I spent the first part of the afternoon attempting to flat-out ignore him, and when that didn't work, I switched to cutting him off as soon as he starting talking, with variations of "Go *away*, Evan." But nothing worked. He was relentless.

The second rehearsal ended, I booked it out of there and went straight home, relieved to finally be free from all of it, if only until tomorrow.

I should have known that wouldn't be the end of it. I was in the kitchen helping Dad with dinner when Evan showed up on my doorstep.

Papa answered the door; from the next room over, I heard their whole conversation.

"Hi, Evan," Papa said.

"Hi, Mr. Freeman."

"Oh, you can call me Seth."

"Cool. Is Lucy around?"

I tried to wave at Papa, to get his attention and mime that I wasn't here, but he didn't see me. I still hadn't told them that Evan and I had broken up, so Papa didn't know that he was doing anything wrong when he invited Evan in for dinner.

They came into the kitchen together. "Did you know that Evan here has never had pizza on the grill before? We are going to have to fix that immediately," Papa said. But his lighthearted demeanor faded when he saw my face. "You okay, Lu?"

I was gripping onto my knife so tightly my fingers were going numb. "Don't you ever give *up*?" I said.

"I just want to talk to you," Evan said.

I glanced at my dads, who were watching us in confusion. I wasn't going to have this conversation in front of them. All I needed was yet more people hounding me about my seemingly nonexistent reason for breaking up with Evan.

"Fine. I'm going out," I told them. "Save me some pizza." I tossed the knife onto the counter, and pulled Evan out of the house.

We got in my car, but I didn't drive anywhere.

"All right, you win. Let's talk," I said.

"You owe me an explanation—" he began.

"No, actually, I don't. You're the one who owes me an explanation."

"For what?"

"For harassing me—no, *stalking* me—to no end. What the hell, Evan?"

"I just want to understand."

I groaned in frustration and slammed my hands against the steering wheel. "We've been through this."

He didn't say anything.

"Evan, we were only together a month."

We glared at each other, deadlocked. I was prepared to stay there all night if that was what it took to get it into his thick skull.

But it didn't take nearly that long. A couple of minutes, maybe. I don't know what caused it, but out of nowhere something in Evan's face changed. He broke my stare, his expression grew softer, and he let out a long, heaving sigh.

"You're right."

"I am?"

"Yeah. I'm really sorry, Lucy. About all of this," he mumbled. "I just...I just needed to know why everyone always leaves me."

Okay, this conversation was not going at all the way I'd anticipated. "What do you mean?"

He cleared his throat and looked down at his lap. "First my dad bails on me and my mom for a twenty-seven-year-old spin instructor. Then Sarah goes away to school and all of a sudden starts acting like I'm some child who she never took seriously. So I come here and meet you and think maybe things aren't so bad after all, and then you dump me too. I just want to understand what about me is so entirely repellent, so I can stop doing that."

My heart was breaking. I'd thought I was protecting him but the whole time I was hurting him more than I could have imagined. "Oh, Evan." I placed a hand on his shoulder. "I'm sorry."

He looked up at me. "Please. I promise I'll leave you alone and never talk to you ever again if you just tell me the real reason why you don't want to be with me."

I hesitated.

I was certain of only two things.

One: I couldn't keep dodging his question with half-answers. I hadn't realized how much that was wounding him, and I wasn't going to do that again.

Two: I should absolutely make up a lie. *I'm not ready for another serious relationship* or *I'm still in love with Ty* or *my grades have been slipping and I need to spend all my free time studying.* That was the smart thing to do. But I didn't want to lie to him. My life was already complicated enough without having to keep track of deceptions.

That tiny voice, in the far recesses of my head, was saying, *Tell him the truth. What's the worst that could happen?*

I honestly didn't know what the worst that could happen was, and I didn't want to think about it. But as I studied Evan, and the little voice grew louder, I considered the possibility that maybe I *could* tell him the truth. He'd opened up to me, and it had gone okay. Maybe I could do the same.

I suddenly knew that if I was ever going to tell anyone, now was the moment.

"Lucy?"

I looked him straight in the eyes and took a deep, frightened breath. "If I tell you the truth, do you swear not to tell another soul as long as you live?"

His eyebrows crinkled together. "Of course."

"Say you promise."

He nodded. "I promise."

I couldn't believe I was about to do this. But it all came out anyway. "Back in September, I was going through some stuff. Ty dumped me, Lisa came back, all that. It all seems so dumb now, but I was really upset. So Courtney and Max and I went to the city and got really drunk and I ended up going home with this random guy."

He nodded to show he was following, but he was clearly confused as to what any of this had to do with him.

"Afterward, I went and got tested for STIs. And…" I took one more deep breath. "I tested positive for HIV." It was the first time I'd said it out loud, and as the words escaped my mouth, I felt a shift somewhere deep inside me. Like one teeny-tiny shackle was unlatched, and I was one small step closer to freedom.

Evan's eyes grew wide and his hand flew to his mouth. "Oh my god."

I watched his face carefully, searching for symptoms of what he could possibly be thinking. But I couldn't read his expression.

"Does anyone else know?" he asked after a minute.

"No."

"Not even your dads?"

"No."

"Lucy, you have to tell them."

"No, I don't. You don't understand. It would kill them."

"But they're your parents. They should know." His eyes darted to the house.

"Listen, Evan," I said, starting to get worried. "You can't tell them. You can't tell anyone. You promised."

"But that was before I knew what you were going to say. I had no idea…"

"I only told you because I felt like I owed you the truth. But no one else needs to know. It's my business."

He looked back and forth between the house's kitchen window and my face. Finally, he said, "Okay. I won't tell anyone."

I exhaled. "Thank you."

We sat there quietly for a few minutes.

"Well," Evan said eventually, "I guess I should go."

"Wait." I reached out and I grabbed onto his arm. I didn't want him to go.

And then, as if in slow motion, he looked at my hand gripped around his bare forearm, my skin against his, and he jerked away from my touch.

"Oh," I said, understanding. He was frightened of me. My insides felt like they were being ripped apart by steel claws.

He ran his hands through his hair nervously. "I, uh, don't know why I did that."

"I do," I said quietly, hurt. "You know, you can't catch it that way."

"Yeah. That was stupid. I'm really sorry." His face was red.

"And that's exactly why I don't want anyone else to know. I don't want everyone looking at me the way you're looking at me right now. Just go. It's fine."

His hand was on the door handle. "Wait, what were you going to say?"

Oh, I don't know, just that I still really like you, and was hoping that now that you knew the truth maybe we could give us another try? Chalk it up to temporary insanity.

"Nothing. Forget it," I said.

"Okay. If you're sure…"

"Yup. So…I'll see you at school, I guess."

"Yeah." He paused for a brief moment. "Bye, Lucy." And then he was gone.

I shouldn't have told him.

16
Maybe I Like it This Way

The next day, in Andre's homeroom, the room was more alive than I was. Conversations. Line-running. Monologue-practicing. Affectionate couples. Ty and Elyse, sharing a chair, legs wrapped around each other.

Everything was normal.

It was me that was out of place.

I sat in my usual seat next to Max and Court.

"What's up?" I said. My voice sounded off, like an inflectionless robot.

"Not much," Courtney said, shrugging. "What's up with you?"

"Nothing."

And that was it. We fell into the first awkward silence of our twelve-year friendship.

Evan came in just after the bell and, rather than sit by us like he always did, took a seat near the door. I kept my eyes on him throughout the period, waiting for him to look my way, but he kept his attention directed at the front of the room. He was out of there as soon as homeroom ended.

I searched for him between classes, but he wasn't in any of his usual places. He wasn't at lunch, either. But Courtney and Max were, and they may as well have been wearing t-shirts that said "AWK-" and "-WARD." Everything felt forced. Suddenly we didn't have anything to talk about, and the entire period skulked by in a series of discomfited silences and small-talk attempts.

I never thought I'd be eager to get away from my best friends.

I finally saw Evan at rehearsal. I'd already gotten our swords off the prop table, and I handed him his. "Hi," I said, resisting the unbelievably powerful urge to run away.

His kept his gaze focused on the floor. "Thanks. For the, uh, sword."

"No problem. You've been like Houdini all day."

"I…I've been busy."

Yeah, busy avoiding me. I tried to keep my voice light. "Ready for combat, sir Tybalt?"

"Oh, um. Sure," he said.

But combat rehearsal didn't go well. How were Evan and I supposed to be in sync when he wouldn't even look me in the eye or come within two feet of me? We stumbled through the choreography like our feet were bricks. Andre was so unhappy with our performance, he sent everyone home early. Evan couldn't get out of there fast enough.

• • •

The days turned into a week, then two. Halloween came and went. I barely noticed. I became withdrawn from everyone, everything.

I kept forgetting my lines and missing my cues. The show was set to open in less than a month, and thanks to my distance and Evan's revulsion of me, it was shaping up to be the worst Eleanor Drama production in history. After a few days of absolutely atrocious rehearsals, Andre asked me to stay late.

"I don't know what's going on with you, Lucy, but you need to pull it together. *Now*," he said.

"I know," I muttered.

"No, I don't think you do. I'm *this close* to recasting your role. If that happens, you're out. For good. I know you don't want that."

"No," I agreed. I wasn't supposed to want that. Right? But it was hard to muster up the appropriate reaction. The old me, the me that cared about things like the drama club, was locked away deep inside my head, but she wasn't the one in charge anymore. It was that unnamed thing that entered my body way back at the very first utterance of the word *positive*. It was growing and festering and whispering *what's the point?* over and over again with every heartbeat. And it was right—there was no point to any of it.

Andre wasn't the only one who confronted me.

Elyse sauntered up to me in the women's dressing room, her sparkly skirt swishing over her Stairmaster-perfected thighs. "You know, it's a good thing I transferred to this school," she announced, right in front of all the other cast members.

"Why is that, Elyse?" I said, humoring her.

"Well, it's one thing for you to ruin *your* four scenes, but just imagine if you'd been cast as Juliet. They'd have to cancel the show!"

I stared at her, humiliated, trying to conjure up an appropriate comeback. But I came up with nothing.

"Don't feel bad, though," she continued mock-sweetly, clearly enjoying herself. "Lots of people are considered 'good actors'"—yes, she did the air quotes—"when they're kids and then just can't hack it when it's time to be taken seriously. But don't worry, it's not like you won't be able to have a career in the theater—I'm sure there's a box office or usher job with your name on it." Her phone rang. "It's Ty. I have to take this." She turned and swished back the way she came.

God, what did Ty *see* in her? And how could Max call *me* a bitch when *that* bitch was walking around like the sun shone out the back of her thong?

I glanced intuitively over at Courtney. She just kept putting on makeup, like she was completely ignorant of what had just happened. But there was no way she hadn't heard. I took her silence the only way it could be interpreted—she agreed with Elyse.

I started spending lunches by myself in the empty auditorium, and I sat in the back of the room, alone, in homeroom. Courtney and Max stopped talking to me altogether. Our threesome had become a twosome. Who knew our friendship could turn out to be so precarious. It was surreal, seeing them in the halls and in homeroom and at rehearsals, but not being able to cross the invisible barrier that had formed between us. There was a part of me that was always aware of them, that perked up when they were in close proximity, but that part was completely detached from the part of me that was supposed to care. So we went on pretending like we had never been more than classmates.

At home, things weren't much better.

Lisa's belly was getting bigger, but she stopped asking me for baby names after a while, because all I'd been able to come up with was Lisa Jr. And why should I have to name her baby, anyway? Couldn't she do *anything* herself?

But unlike my friends and pseudo-mother, my dads couldn't just ignore my behavior. At first, it was a series of "Are you okay's" and "What's on your mind's" and shared, worried glances. But as it became more apparent to them that whatever I was going through was more than a phase, they upped their game.

I came home after a dreadful Sunday afternoon rehearsal to find Dad and Papa in the living room, the TV and stereo off, the room quiet. They had been waiting for me.

I glanced at the stack of library books on the coffee table, and back to my parents.

"What is this?" I asked.

"Lucy, sit down," Dad said, gesturing to the chair positioned across from them.

"Actually, I'm gonna go to my room—I have homework."

"No," Dad said firmly. "Sit."

I cursed under my breath and dragged myself over to the chair. "Fine. What?"

"Lu," Papa began. "Your father and I are concerned about your behavior as of late."

"We understand that it's difficult being a teenager, and we can only imagine what it's like being a teenage girl, but we want you to know that you can always talk to us. About anything," Dad said.

There was a silence. I stared at the abstract pattern on Dad's designer rug.

"Well? Is there anything you'd like to share with us?" Papa said.

"No, thanks," I mumbled. The more I stared, the more the lines on the rug blurred together.

They looked at each other.

"Lucy," Dad said, with more of an edge to his voice now, "we received a phone call from your director. He told us you haven't been focused in rehearsals, and that you've had some sort of falling out with Max and Courtney. What is going on with you? This isn't normal."

The carpet design disappeared entirely and became just another distorted mess in my head.

"We're worried about you, Lu. So now we're going to have to take some measures," Papa continued.

That word caught my attention. "Measures?"

"We'd like you to talk to a psychiatrist. Medication in conjunction with regular therapy has been proven to help with depression. It's also probably a good idea to have some tests run to check for any medical abnormalities that might be altering your mood."

I shook my head. "No way."

"We have no choice, Lucy," Dad said. "Things have to change."

I couldn't do what they wanted me to do. If I had those medical tests done, it would be no time at all before they learned the truth. I glanced, panicked, at the pile of books. "What are those?" I asked.

"I got them out of the library for you," said Papa. "I thought maybe it would help to know that whatever you're going through, you're not alone."

I read through the titles. The subjects spanned every possible teenage problem except the one I was actually dealing with. Body image issues, sexual confusion, drug and alcohol abuse, unwanted pregnancy…

Nothing about contracting HIV at sixteen from a drunken one-night stand. That's because Papa was wrong—I *was* alone in this.

But I had to do something. I stood up and lifted the hefty stack of books. "Thanks," I said. "I'm going to go look through these. I'm sure you're right—they probably will help." I went up to my room before they could stop me again.

• • •

I couldn't sleep. Every time I closed my eyes, haunting memories filled the darkness. And not just any memories—blood-themed ones. I'd never realized it before, but blood narrated my life.

The thin trickle, so dark it was almost black, that ran down my shin after I fell off my bike when I was five.

The first time I cut myself shaving my legs.

The blood-stained tissue that I pulled away from my face after being accidentally kicked in the nose by Regina Arnold during dance class at theater camp three summers ago.

The tiny bead of red that sat on my fingertip after I pricked myself with the needle I was using to sew together a stuffed elephant for Courtney's sixteenth birthday gift.

The three vials of thick crimson that Marie filled for my STI tests.

I jolted upright in my bed.

One for your syphilis test and one for hepatitis C. And one for your HIV confirmatory test if necessary, Marie had said.

Oh my god. I may have still had an out.

I leapt out of bed and dug around in my purse until I found what I was looking for. The sheet of paper that Marie had given me that held my anonymous patient code and the phone number to call for my results. The paper I'd forgotten all about the moment Diane had said the word *positive*.

I dialed the number. As it rang, my heart swelled with hope. Maybe everything I'd been through in the last few weeks was for nothing. Maybe it was all a big mistake. That would be okay, I wouldn't hold Marie or Diane or the clinic responsible. A few weeks of misery seemed a small price to pay to be given my life back.

The clinic's voicemail clicked on. Of course there wouldn't be someone there at three a.m. I carefully smoothed out the paper and crawled back into bed. But I still didn't sleep. I couldn't think about anything but the possibility that I wasn't actually positive. Mistakes must happen all the time—otherwise they wouldn't need to do the confirmatory test, right?

There was still a chance. Why hadn't I seen that before?

• • •

I called the clinic again at nine, but they were closed for Veterans Day. I'd have to wait until tomorrow to get my good news.

School was closed too, but we still had rehearsal. My face felt peculiar as I got ready to go. And then I realized—I was smiling for the first time in ages. I gave my dads each a peck on the cheek before I left the house. They were stunned by my sudden transformation. They must have thought their library books really did the trick.

As I drove to the school, a little fire ignited in my belly. Today was going to be a good day.

Right away, I apologized to Andre. "I know it's no excuse, but I've been going through a lot lately. I'm really sorry that it's affected our rehearsals, but it's all better now. You don't have to worry anymore, okay?"

I don't know if it was my words themselves or the positive energy surrounding them, but Andre threw his arms around me. "Thank Jesus!" he said. "This show wouldn't have been the same without you—you're our little star, missy!"

I laughed. "Thanks, Andre."

Rehearsal went brilliantly. I actually had *fun*. Andre had nothing but positive feedback for me, the groans of exasperation from my castmates vanished, and Elyse's face looked like she'd bit into a lemon—that's how I really knew I was back.

The only thing that didn't go smoothly was the swordfight. Evan was still skittish around me. He didn't realize that everything had changed, that tomorrow I would get my official results and I'd be able to tell him that I didn't have HIV after all and that everything would finally go back to normal.

• • •

Tuesday morning, at nine a.m. exactly, I told my pre-calc teacher I had to go to the bathroom, and I slipped out of the school and into my car. I called the clinic number again, and this time a real live person answered.

"I'm calling for my test results," I said, every word filled with optimism.

"Patient number?" she asked, sounding bored out of her skull.

I gave her the number and waited.

"Chlamydia, negative. Gonorrhea, negative. Syphilis, negative. Hepatitis C, negative."

I waited for her to give me the HIV results, but she didn't say anything else.

"Is there anything else I can help you with?" the lady asked after a moment.

"Um, yes, I need my HIV test results."

"Didn't they give those results to you while you were here in the clinic?"

"Yeah, but they needed to do a confirmatory test."

There was a slight pause. "If your rapid test was reactive, the social worker should have told you what to do to get your confirmatory results."

Oh. I obviously didn't stick around long enough to get that information from Diane. "I…don't…uh…remember what she said."

The lady sighed loudly. "Take down this number. You'll need to speak with a social worker directly. Do you have a pen?"

I scrambled around in my backpack for a pen and notebook, and then took down the number. "But wait," I said. "Do you have my results in front of you right now?"

"Yes, ma'am, I do."

"Well then, can't you just tell me them? Why do I have to call someone else?"

"I'm not authorized to do that."

I was beginning to get upset. "What do you mean? You're authorized to give me my other test results. Why not this one?"

"I'm sorry, I can't answer that. Have a nice day." She hung up.

What the hell?

I dialed the social worker's number, my pulse racing.

"Diane Sullivan," she answered on the first ring.

I cleared my throat. "Um, hi, this is Lucy Moore." I realized too late that I wasn't supposed to use my last name. "I was in there back in October—"

"Lucy! Yes, I remember," Diane said. "How are you doing?"

"I'm fine," I lied. "I'm just calling for my confirmatory results."

"Well, we usually ask our clients to come in person to receive their results. Would you like to schedule an appointment now? I have several openings this week."

"No, I want to know now."

"Lucy, it really is better if we speak in person."

I hesitated. "Why?"

"It's standard procedure—"

My grip tightened around the phone. "It's because I'm positive, isn't it?"

There was a tension-filled pause. "We ask everyone to come in, regardless of their results."

"I'm pretty sure you're not legally allowed to withhold my results from me." Having a lawyer for a father came in handy sometimes.

Diane gave a tiny, yielding sigh. "Do you have your client number available? For confidentiality reasons, I can't give you any results without it."

I read it to her, the paper and my voice shaking. I heard Diane's fingers typing the number into a computer.

"Lucy, your HIV result is positive."

I dropped the phone in my lap and brought my forehead to the steering wheel.

The hope I'd been clinging to since three o'clock yesterday morning evaporated.

I waited for the nausea, for the panic, for the demons' resurgence. I waited for the streak of denial, for the compulsion to lash out in violence. I waited for any perceptible reaction at all, but nothing happened.

And then I realized. Nothing was happening because inside, I was already dead.

"Lucy?" Diane's tinny distant voice was calling to me. "Are you there?"

I took the length of five deep, long breaths.

"Hello? Lucy?"

Slowly, I picked up the phone and brought it back to my ear. "I'm here."

"What are you feeling right now?"

"Nothing," I said truthfully.

"It's important for you to understand that with proper medical care and support, people with HIV can lead very productive lives," she said.

"You have to say that."

"I don't. I say it because it's true. I've been doing this a long time, Lucy. I know many people with HIV who live quite normally."

"Well, I'm not one of them."

"You can be," she said.

"No. I can't." My voice was rising. "You don't understand. How am I supposed to care about *normal* things like high school when I'm slowly being killed from the inside out? How am I supposed to be *normal* when the first person I told ran for the hills the second the words came out of my mouth?"

"I'm very sorry to hear that happened to you. But I'm sure you have many people in your life who will support you. A trusted friend or family member, maybe?"

"No. I'm not telling anyone else."

"Having a reliable support system in place is a key factor in living a full, happy life, Lucy. I'd encourage you to reconsider. In the meantime, we have many group meetings here at the clinic, and I'd also really like to schedule a one-on-one in-person appointment with you."

The dim ring of the bell sounded from within the school's walls.

"I have to go," I said quickly, grateful for an excuse to end the conversation. "Bye."

"Wait, Lucy—"

I hung up the phone. The *normal* world was calling for me.

17

Sixteen Going on Seventeen

Lucy Moore as I had always known her ceased to exist. Instead, I was Mercutio. Rehearsals were my only link to the living. On stage, I got to be someone else entirely. I didn't have to be me anymore, and I craved that time away from myself. So I was able to keep my promise to Andre, and rehearsals continued to go well.

When I wasn't at rehearsal, I played the guitar. When I was immersed in a song, the music escorted my pain away, if only temporarily.

And I don't know where it came from, but something amazing happened—I started writing songs. I'd never written my own stuff before. Whenever I'd tried, the only thing that came out were other people's songs long ago stenciled on my brain. I'd begun to think there was nothing original inside me at all. But suddenly, I was filling notebook upon notebook with melodies and lyrics.

It was Friday night and I was alone, of course. My little desk lamp with the purple shade cast its dull light over my room. Dad and Papa were out at an art show (having realized their little library book enchantment had worn off, they'd tried to get me to go with them, insisting it would do me good to get out of the house, but I'd just kept strumming my guitar absentmindedly and eventually they gave up and left me alone), and Lisa had left shortly after they had, though I didn't bother asking her where she was going. I was sitting in my favorite spot on my floor, my back against the bedframe, guitar in my lap. I played for hours, the six strings combining with my voice, the sound so big the four walls of my bedroom couldn't contain it—it spilled under the door and out the windows so that the only sound in the world was this music.

I was so lost in it, playing so intensely, that it was a long time before I noticed that my fingers had actually started to bleed.

The song cut off and I stared at my bloody hand. I probably should have run to the bathroom to clean and bandage them right away, but I was mesmerized, watching the little red beads pulse and ooze from my fingertips. The blood spilled from my fingers, pooled around my cuticles, stained my nails, collected slowly in my palms.

So this was what it looked like: my new blood. The thing that was keeping me alive and killing me at the same time. It looked normal enough. Red. Plasmic. Wet.

The gashes were deep, on all five of my right hand's fingers. The blood dripped onto the wooden body of my guitar. I didn't wipe it off. Instead, I started playing again. I didn't care that I was making the open wounds even worse, and I didn't care that blood was getting all over the strings.

I played and sang and wrote till I passed out, and woke up the next morning still fully dressed, hugging my bloody guitar, scabs forming on my fingers.

It was November 17th. My golden birthday. I was seventeen years old today.

It was a Saturday, so luckily I didn't have to go to school and suffer through all the smiling faces wishing me a happy birthday. Today was the first of my limited reserve of birthdays left, and there was nothing "happy" about it.

I shuffled downstairs and found that my dads had woken up early to make me my traditional birthday breakfast. A giant stack of alternating pancakes and homemade waffles, covered in whipped cream, chocolate syrup, and chocolate sprinkles, with a big fat birthday candle stuck in the top. I'd assumed this year we'd be forgoing the annual calorie-fest in light of my recent withdrawal from life, but I guess it was going to take a lot more than a severe case of depression to make my dads cancel their only daughter's birthday festivities.

"Happy birthday, Lucy!" they cheered as I entered the kitchen. They were wearing party hats and blowing into noise-makers.

I sank into a chair. "Coffee?" I said, cradling my head in my hands.

"Coming right up! Anything for the birthday girl!" Papa said.

"Where's Lisa?" I mumbled.

"Still sleeping. The pregnancy's really making her exhausted these days," Dad said. "Should we wake her up? This is your first birthday with all of us under the same roof, you know."

"And only seventeen years too late," I muttered under my breath.

"What's that, honey?"

"Nothing. No, don't wake her."

Papa placed my birthday feast along with my *Rent* mug filled with black coffee in front of me.

And then they sang. "Happy birthday to you, happy birthday to you…"

They waited for me to blow out the candle. "Make a wish, Lu!" they urged.

Suddenly, everything came to a grinding halt. *Make a wish.* As if it were that easy. As if I hadn't been ceaselessly wishing since that day at the clinic. As if something as innocent as a childish birthday wish would right all my wrongs. As if the one thing I wanted wasn't impossible.

Out of nowhere, I began to cry, the tears running down my cheeks at the exact same speed as the wax that was dripping down the still-lit candle.

Caught off guard, my dads immediately rushed to my side and put their arms around me.

"Lucy? What is it?" Dad asked anxiously.

It was *everything*. Becoming another year older, my brittle, scabbed fingers, the *Rent* mug, my dads' smiling faces…it was all too much.

And then the physics of it all became suddenly clear: the only way to keep from sinking was to unburden myself of the weight.

"I have to tell you something," I blurted out before I even knew what I was doing.

They pulled back and looked at each other. Dad sat on my left, Papa on my right, and they waited. I could only imagine what was going through their heads right now, but I knew that they weren't expecting what I was about to say.

I finally knew what to wish for: *Please don't hate me, please don't hate me, please don't hate me,* I thought.

And then I said it. "I have HIV." It's amazing how much weight three small words, five tiny syllables, can hold.

The only sound in the whole house was the crackling of the candle. I blew it out.

18
You'll Never Walk Alone

There was no going back now.

I held my breath.

My fathers' faces were so blank, so perplexed, that at first I thought they hadn't heard me. And I truly didn't know if I could say it a second time. But they just didn't know what to do with what I'd just said.

After a while, the blankness melted away and was replaced by disbelief. Papa even let out a miniscule chuckle, as if he thought I was kidding. The first real sign of actual comprehension was the twitching of Dad's fingers, and then the eventual reaching out and clasping of Papa's hand.

The reality and gravity of my words began to sink in. No one said a word. Dad's face crumpled, his Adam's apple bobbing with each deliberate gulp of air, his eyes filling with tears. I was stunned—I'd never seen him cry before. No matter what we'd gone through, he'd always been my rock. He released Papa's hand and collapsed against me, sobbing. Suddenly he was the child, and I was the parent. He was shattered, and it was all I could do to remain strong—keeping my own breakdown at arm's length—and hold him, afraid to let go and watch the pieces fall away.

Papa, on the other hand, was mad. Enraged, actually. His face was beet red, veins popping through his forehead. He knocked over his chair and stormed out of the house, slamming the door so hard the kitchen cabinets rattled.

I released my trapped breath. My birthday wish had failed—Papa hated me.

"Dad?" I whispered. "Dad, talk to me."

There was no change. The crying continued. The shoulder of my T-shirt grew wet with his tears.

"Dad," I tried again. "Please. Stop crying."

Still nothing. Did he even hear me?

"Dad, you're really heavy. My arms are going numb."

That got through to him. He weakly sat back in his own chair and blew his nose into a Happy Birthday napkin.

"Are you okay?" I asked softly.

It took a minute for him to find his voice. "How did this happen?" he said finally.

I sighed. "Does it really matter?"

"Lucy." He met my gaze. "Of course it matters."

I nodded. "Yeah, I guess it does." I told him the whole story, not editing anything out; there was no point in lying now. As I spoke, I couldn't help feeling that I was waiting on his verdict, like the emotional breakdown was just an initial gut reaction, but after he'd had time to digest all the facts then he'd decide how he really felt. So I didn't mind that it took a long time to relay the whole wretched truth—I figured the longer I talked, the longer I could prolong his judgment.

When I finished, I hung my head and said, "I'm so sorry, Daddy."

Dad was silent. He was staring down at his lap; I couldn't read the thoughts behind his eyes.

This day's black fate on more days doth depend.
This but begins the woe others must end.

When he did speak, his words surprised me. He reached over and squeezed my hand tightly and said, "No, Lucy, I'm sorry."

I blinked. "For what?"

"For allowing Lisa to come back here…"

"Dad," I cut him off, "this is *not* your fault. It's mine."

"Let me finish. I *am* sorry for letting Lisa come back. I should have known better. And I'm also sorry that you felt like you had to keep this from us. It's been eating at you, and we should have known."

"Dad, please, stop blam—"

"Lucy," he continued, as though I hadn't even spoken, "you deserve so much better than this life." His voice broke and he paused to steady himself. "Things aren't going to be easy for you.

But your father and I love you so very much, and we are going to be there for you every step of the way. Do you understand?"

He knew the truth, and he still loved me. I believed him when he said he loved me and would be there for me, but I didn't believe that Papa felt the same way.

"I don't think Papa would agree with you," I said flatly.

"He does," Dad said. "He just needs some time."

"I've never seen him that mad. He's going to hate me forever."

"Lucy, listen to me." Dad grabbed my shoulders and looked me directly in the eyes. "I know Seth better than anyone. He doesn't hate you—he's mad at himself."

"For what?"

"He thinks he's failed you. And he's right. It's our job to protect you—from everything from monsters under the bed to…things like this."

I noticed that he couldn't bring himself to say the actual word.

"We tried," he continued. "We did everything we could think of to keep you safe. I always thought, if anything, you'd get pregnant. But Papa—*this* was always his worst fear."

"It was?"

Dad nodded.

"But why?" It wasn't like this sort of thing happened all that often to girls like me.

"Do you remember Patrick?"

Patrick. Our old family friend. I hadn't thought about him in years. All I really remembered about him was that he gave me my very first Broadway album—the original cast recording of *Beauty and the Beast*—and he spent Christmannukahs with us when I was young.

"Only a little," I admitted.

"Patrick was Seth's best friend in the world. They met in second grade and were inseparable ever since—kind of like you and Max and Courtney. He had his share of problems, but he loved Seth and he adored you. We didn't find out until very late that he had AIDS. I don't even think he knew until those last months."

A memory was dislodged. I was about six, and Papa was so sad. I asked him what was wrong, and he told me that Patrick had died. He'd had a disease. I asked if I could catch Patrick's disease. Papa took me into his arms and promised me I couldn't.

Okay, now Papa's reaction made a whole lot more sense.

Dad and I spent the rest of the day at his art gallery. They were closed on Saturdays, and we set up a picnic on the floor and ate falafel sandwiches and drank milkshakes surrounded by all the works of art.

I don't know how he did it, considering it was the only thing both of us were thinking about, but Dad didn't mention it again for the rest of the day. Instead we talked about the play and we talked about the documentary he'd just seen about a guy who decided to live for an entire year without earning or using money and we talked about the vegetable garden he wanted to plant in the spring.

We walked around the gallery, pausing in front of each painting and sculpture. Dad told me about the artists and what the intention was behind some of the more abstract pieces. I couldn't believe how much they were selling some of them for—my favorite painting, an enormous canvas covered in different shades of blue, with paintbrush bristles dried into the paint strokes, was sixty-five thousand dollars.

As the sun started to set outside the gallery doors, Dad surreptitiously glanced at his phone. He'd texted Papa before we'd left the house, letting him know where we'd be, and I knew he'd been hoping he would show up. We both were.

"Still no response, huh?"

The corners of Dad's mouth turned down the slightest bit. "He'll come around," he said, tucking the phone back in his pocket.

"If you say so," I said.

"Lucy, have I ever told you about the time I told my parents I was gay?"

I thought back. "I don't think so."

He nodded. "I was seventeen. The prom was coming up and my parents asked me one night at dinner if there were any girls at school that I wanted to ask. I was so taken off guard I distinctly remember choking and spitting out a mouthful of peas. I'd thought they'd known I was gay; I'd always assumed it was obvious. I'd never shown any interest whatsoever in girls and the walls of my bedroom were covered with pictures of Luke Perry and Johnny Depp."

I giggled and Dad smiled.

"So I shook my head and said, 'Uh, I'm gay. I thought you knew that.' I was so casual about it. But they weren't. Apparently they hadn't had the slightest idea—and they were not happy. My mother immediately started praying and my father actually kicked me out of the house, shouting that no son of his was going to be a faggot. I had to stay with friends for over a month."

"But Grandma and Grandpa are members of PFLAG! They love Papa!"

"They do now. But it took them a while to get used to the idea."

"Whoa."

"The point is, Lucy, that they came around. And so will Papa. Just give him a little time," Dad said.

We threw away our food containers and packed up to go home. "Dad?" I said as we walked to the car. "Thanks for today. It actually wasn't such a terrible birthday, all things considered."

He took my hand. "I love you, honey."

"Love you too." I let those words linger in the air for a moment. "Oh, and one more thing—can you not tell Lisa about any of this? Or anyone else?"

He studied me for a moment. "Of course," he said, and we drove home.

19
Sunday

Papa didn't get home until the next morning. Dad and I were sitting at the table, stewing, our untouched breakfast congealing in front of us, when he shuffled in. He was still dressed in yesterday's rumpled clothes and his face was all stubbly. Dad breathed a long sigh of relief. I watched and waited.

He hovered in the doorway, pausing, looking at me. When he finally came in, he scooted my chair out so I was facing him, and then he kneeled down on the kitchen floor tile and flung his arms around me.

It was the first time I felt like things might actually be okay.

"Dad told me about Patrick," I whispered.

He held on a little longer, then pulled back to look at me. "Lucy Rose Moore," he said firmly, "you are not Patrick. Patrick was an idiot."

Well, I wasn't expecting *that*.

Papa continued. "Patrick was irresponsible and reckless and didn't know the first thing about taking care of himself. You are smart and young and have the whole world in front of you. You are *not* Patrick," he said again. I didn't know if he was trying to convince me or himself.

It was then that Lisa came downstairs. She took one look at Papa and said, "Christ, Seth, you look bloody awful," before helping herself to a gigantic bowl of cereal with a heaping tablespoon of sugar on top.

"Good morning to you too, Lisa," Papa said, shooting her a loathsome glance.

"Lucy, Seth," Dad stepped in, "why don't we leave Lisa to her breakfast and go sit on the back porch?"

"It's about forty degrees outside, Adam."

"So?" Dad replied, giving him a pointed look and nodding his head in Lisa's direction. "Thank you," I mouthed to Dad as the three of us left the kitchen.

"All right, what was that all about?" Papa asked after we were all safely outside in the crisp morning air.

"Lucy has requested that we don't discuss any of this in front of Lisa."

"I don't want her to know," I said.

Papa nodded, thinking. "She would probably be less than understanding."

"Yeah, but that's not exactly it. I don't want anyone to know."

"No one?"

"No one."

"What about your friends?"

"I told Evan. It didn't go well."

"Oh." Papa frowned. "What about Courtney and Max?"

I shook my head. "I'm not telling anyone else."

"What about—"

"Papa, I'm not telling anyone. End of story."

"You may change your mind about that," Dad said. "But now that the three of us are together, we need to figure out what we're going to do next."

A slight tremor rumbled inside me. "What do you mean?"

"First, we need to find you a good doctor. You need to go on medication," Dad said.

"And regular therapy is going to be crucial as well," Papa continued. "I'll make some calls, ask around."

It seemed the idyllic let's-not-talk-about-it arrangement from yesterday was long gone. I shook my head. "No way. No doctors, no therapy."

They stared at me.

"What are you talking about?" Dad asked.

"I don't want any of that. I went online, Dad, I know what this thing is going to do to me. I'd just rather live my life normally for as long as I can before I have to deal with any of that stuff." I didn't think it necessary to mention that my life had already lost all semblance of normalcy.

"But, Lucy, doctors and medication and therapy are the things that are going to *allow* you to live a normal life. Don't you understand?" Dad said.

"I don't care. I don't want it," I repeated stubbornly, arms folded over my chest.

So quickly I didn't even see him do it, Papa crossed the porch and grabbed my face. "You listen to me, young lady. You are a minor, and we are your parents. Therefore, you will do what we say. Got it?"

My eyes grew wide. Papa never spoke to me like that—he always took my side. But clearly something had changed in him. "But—"

"This is not up for negotiation, Lucy," Papa said, releasing his grip on me. "You are not giving up."

"Papa," I said slowly and calmly. "What is HIV?"

"Don't you know?" he asked.

"Of course I know. But I want to hear it from you."

He remained silent.

"Fine, I'll say it. It's the virus that causes AIDS. And what is AIDS?"

I waited again for him to respond, but he didn't, so again I answered my own question.

"It's a disease that tears your body apart until you die." I paused to clear my throat and collect myself. "Papa, don't you get it? I have HIV, and someday I'm going to have AIDS, and someday after that I'm going to die."

I heard Dad's sniffling, but I didn't remove my gaze from Papa's face.

He stared back at me with fiery eyes and a set jaw. "Not on my watch," he said.

• • •

That evening as I was getting ready for bed, they came up to my room.

"I did some investigating," Papa said, "and found a doctor in the city that comes highly recommended. I'm going to call first thing tomorrow to get you an appointment. And this," he said, handing me a stack of computer printouts, "is information about different therapists, group meetings, and support centers in Westchester and Manhattan. You can review them and decide which ones you'd like to try."

"I don't want to try any of them," I mumbled.

"Well, you should have thought about that before going home with some guy you didn't know, shouldn't you?" Papa snapped back.

I gasped. I'd assumed Dad would tell him the whole story, but the last thing I expected was for him to throw it back in my face like that.

He swallowed. "I'm sorry, Lu," he said more softly. "I didn't mean…I don't blame you. It just…would mean a lot to me if you chose a meeting to go to. Or a private therapist, I don't care. But you have to do *something*. Please?"

The picture of Papa's face, frozen in time, as he told me Patrick had died, flickered across my mind.

Why did everything have to be so damn complicated? "Fine," I relented, throwing my hands up in the air. "I'll go. For you. But it's not going to help."

20
One Night Only

Two days later, I was seated on a cold, metal folding chair in the basement of a Methodist church in Greenwich Village. My plan had been to get a seat in the back, but the chairs were arranged in a circle, so there was nowhere to hide. Instead, I chose the seat closest to the door so I could book it out of there as soon as the meeting ended.

There were about a dozen other people in the room: milling about, chatting, laughing, eating their donut holes, and drinking their coffee. They all knew each other already; I was an outsider. I was also the only teenager. I actually may have been the only person under the age of thirty.

Dad and Papa were waiting in a Starbucks around the corner. They'd insisted on escorting me not only to the city but to the front door of the church—they probably thought I would bail on this whole support group idea if left to my own devices. Okay, they were probably right.

I was anxious. I didn't want to tell these people personal things, and I didn't want to listen to their sob stories. Plus they were probably all going to think I was just a dumb kid who had no business encroaching on their intimate little group.

Stop worrying, I told myself. *It'll be fine.*

I chewed on my fingernails.

It was 8:05 now—we were supposed to start at eight. What was the holdup? Why couldn't we just get this damn thing over with already so I could go back to my dads and inform them that it was all a waste of time and that I had no need to ever go back?

At ten after, I was seriously considering leaving. Wasn't there a ten-minute rule or something? Like, if the meeting doesn't begin on time, you all get a free pass to go home? Besides, it wasn't like anyone had even noticed me. I could sneak out now and they'd never know.

Yes. I would go. Run the hell out of this place and never look back.

But just as I'd reached my decision, the big wooden door opened again, and a burst of energy flew into the room.

"Sorry I'm late, guys! My bad!" the woman said. No, woman was the wrong word. She was a young woman, a girl. She couldn't have been much older than I was. She had light brown skin, tight blonde-streaked spiral curls forming a halo around her head, funky eighties-inspired neon pink and green earrings, and hot pink nails. *She* was the one who was running the meeting?

After everyone was seated and the girl had managed to catch her breath, she grinned at each of us. Her teeth were shiny and perfect. "Welcome!"

"Hi, Roxie," a few voices responded back.

"I see we have a new face with us tonight," Roxie said, looking at me. Apparently I wasn't invisible after all. My cheeks turned red at once. "I'm Roxie. What's your name?"

Here we go.

"Lucy," I said.

"Welcome, Lucy. Have you been to a support meeting before?"

"Um, no, this is my first." And last.

"Well, we're happy to have you. Would you like to share?" Roxie asked.

"Share?" I repeated.

"Yeah. Your story, your experience with HIV/AIDS, how you're feeling today…whatever is on your mind."

Everyone looked at me with interest. I couldn't believe they all actually expected me to tell them the most personal details of my life. I didn't *know* them.

"Um," I said, trying to find my voice again. "Actually, I'd rather just listen for now. If that's okay."

Roxie gave me a kind smile. "Of course." Then she turned to the rest of the group. "Who would like to go first? And remember to introduce yourself to Lucy."

A man two seats to my left raised his hand. "I'll go." He was… midthirties, maybe? I couldn't quite tell because his face was oddly concave, like his cheeks had deflated. "I'm Ahmed. It's been a bad week. I was laid off from my job on Monday." There were a few sighs of empathy from the group. "So that means I'm losing my insurance at the end of the month. I don't know what to do—I can't afford my medication without it."

When Ahmed was done speaking, Roxie assured him it would all work out and told him she'd put him in contact with some organizations who would be able to help him get his meds. And he actually seemed more at ease, like he had faith in her ability to help. Who was this girl?

Next, a woman in a big wool sweater and sandals and socks spoke. "I'm June. My daughter had her baby yesterday." There was a wave of congratulations and mazel tovs. June smiled, but only a little. "I went to the hospital to see them. She's beautiful. Andréa Marie. But I wasn't allowed to hold her." She paused and looked down at her lap.

"Why not?" Roxie asked.

"My daughter said she 'didn't want to risk it.'"

"Oh, June," Roxie said. The lady next to June reached out and placed a comforting hand on her back.

I thought back to Evan's reaction when I touched his arm that day in the car. Would it never get better? If people found out I had this disease, would they not want to shake my hand or give me a kiss hello or let me hold their babies?

Several more people shared. Some stories weren't nearly as bad as Ahmed's and June's. One man spoke giddily about a woman he'd just met on an HIV-positive dating site. One woman didn't talk about HIV or AIDS at all—she was just so excited that she'd been asked to be the maid of honor at her best friend's wedding.

And then it was 9:30 and Roxie began to wrap up the meeting. "There is one announcement tonight," she said solemnly. "You may have noticed that Lawrence hasn't been here in a while. I got the sad news this weekend that he passed away last Monday. Before we go, let's have a traditional moment of silence for our friend."

The room went quiet. Some people closed their eyes, others' lips were moving in silent prayer. But I noticed that no one cried. It was like they'd been expecting the news. Maybe Lawrence had been sick for a long time. But then again, Roxie said something about a "tradition." Maybe getting the news that a fellow group member had died wasn't an altogether uncommon occurrence around here. The thought sent a shiver up my spine.

After about a minute, Roxie spoke again. "Thanks, everyone! Remember, there's no meeting this Thursday, but I hope to see you all back here on Friday!"

I'd almost made it to the door when someone caught my arm. "Lucy, hold up."

I turned. It was Roxie.

"Are you going to come back?" She looked at me like she knew I hadn't been planning on it.

"Oh, um, I don't know," I said. "Maybe."

"Well, we're here every Tuesday, Thursday, and Friday. Except this Thursday, you know, because of Thanksgiving."

"Okay," I said, turning back toward the door. "Thanks."

"Lucy?"

"Yes?"

"It's going to be okay. I promise."

What do you say to that?

I just shrugged and left.

21
Sunrise, Sunset

I'd just gotten to school and was stashing my afternoon books in my locker when Courtney walked by, holding hands with Steven Kimani. They were both grinning from ear to ear, and I had barely gotten over the shock of seeing Courtney with a boy when I noticed something else: her mouth was conspicuously metal-free.

I didn't take my eyes off the new couple until they had walked through the double doors at the end of the hall and out of sight. I hadn't known she liked Steven. I hadn't even known they knew each other. How had this happened?

And the braces! Courtney had had braces since sixth grade. Every time she went to the orthodontist she came back in tears because her stubborn overbite forced him to keep pushing back the removal date.

But now it seemed she had the two things she'd always wanted, and I wasn't a part of any of it.

I went up to her in homeroom and spoke to her for the first time in weeks. "Are you going out with Steven Kimani?" I said.

Courtney tried, unsuccessfully, to hide her smile. "Yeah."

"I didn't even know you liked him," I said.

"Well, you haven't exactly been around lately."

"Don't have sex with him, okay?" I blurted out. I don't know what made me say it—it wasn't even an appropriate response to her comment.

A shadow crossed Courtney's face. "Excuse me?"

"Just…trust me. Nothing good can come of it."

"*That's* rich, coming from you!" Her voice was rising. "Go away, Lucy."

Max came into the classroom right then.

He looked from Courtney to me, confused. "What's going on?" he asked.

"Lucy has decided that it's somehow her business whether I do it with Steven or not," Courtney announced, apparently not caring that people were starting to look.

I couldn't help but notice Evan's head snap up. He was listening to our every word.

"Never mind. I'm sorry I said anything," I muttered, and walked out.

Max followed me down the hall.

"What do you want?" I barked, spinning on my heels.

"What exactly did you say to her in there?"

I sighed. "I told her not to have sex with Steven."

Max raised an eyebrow. "Why?"

I gave a noncommittal shrug.

"Listen, Lucy, just because things didn't work out for you and Ty or Evan or that guitar guy doesn't mean it won't for Courtney and Steven. Just stay out of it. Don't ruin this for her."

I shook my head and gave a little sarcastic laugh. "You have absolutely no idea what you're talking about, Max, so why don't *you* stay out of it?"

"Fine," he said.

"Fine," I said back.

We stared each other down there in the empty hallway for a suspended, unblinking moment, and for just the tiniest split-second I thought I saw something sad in his face, something that made me think that maybe he was just as unhappy as I was with the way things between us had deteriorated. But then it was gone, and the anger was back, and we went our separate ways.

• • •

"Lu! Dinner's almost ready!" Dad called.

Reluctantly, I put my guitar down and slogged downstairs. The kitchen smelled amazing.

My dads had decided to forgo the usual full-day Thanksgiving marathon visit to both sides of the family and instead opted for cooking a small dinner at home. Not having to put on a happy-untroubled-teenager act for my grandparents was what I was most thankful for this year.

"The turkey just needs a few more minutes in the oven, and then we'll be ready to eat," Papa said, moving around the place settings to find room for the salad bowl.

I stared at the table. The roasted potatoes were there and so was the stuffing. But there was also an unfamiliar brownish puffy-looking thing in a casserole dish. "What's that?" I asked.

"Lisa made it," Dad said. "Wasn't that nice?"

Nice and *Lisa* weren't two words I'd put in the same sentence. "But what is it?"

"Steak and kidney pie," Lisa said proudly.

"Steak and kidney pie," I repeated, just to make sure I'd heard right. She nodded. "It's English. Try it."

"Sounds…good," I said, and turned my attention back to the actual edible food on the table.

Papa came in with the turkey. "Ta da!" he proclaimed, placing the turkey in the center of the table. "Happy Thanksgiving, everyone!"

The turkey was golden, cooked to perfection, and…revolting. A dead bird was lying in the middle of our kitchen table. A headless carcass, wings folded, innards confiscated. Those visible dark veins used to house pumping blood. A reminder that no matter where I looked, death was following me.

I squeezed my eyes tightly shut and fought the urge to bolt. "Papa," I whispered, "can you get that thing out of here, please?"

"What thing? The turkey?" he asked.

"Yes."

I could only imagine Dad and Papa's silent exchange—they

were probably engaging in a series of concerned glances and word-mouthing. There was some shuffling and clanking of dishes, and then Papa said, "Okay, it's gone."

I opened my eyes and blinked against the light. The turkey was nowhere to be seen. "Thanks," I muttered.

"Lucy—" Dad began gently.

But I stopped him. "Let's eat," I said, and speared a potato with my fork. Dad and Papa seemed to understand that I didn't want to talk about it, but Lisa was another story.

"What the bloody hell was *that* all about?" she said.

Silence. Three pairs of curious eyes pointed my way. No one could explain it but me.

I did the only thing I could think to do. I held my breath and shoveled a heaping spoonful of steak and kidney pie into my mouth. It was the slimiest, most unappetizing thing I had ever tasted, but I forced a smile. "Delicious," I said through a full mouth.

Lisa smiled widely with satisfaction and my dads relaxed.

Papa went into the kitchen to carve his turkey, Dad started spooning out the sides, and the four of us continued our English-inspired Thanksgiving.

• • •

Papa made me go back to the support group on Friday, even though I'd insisted it was pointless.

"Hi, Lucy," June said when I walked in.

"Oh, um, hi," I said. I was surprised she remembered my name; I hadn't even spoken to her on Tuesday.

She smiled at me like she was waiting for me to start a conversation, so I said the first thing that came to mind. "Um, how's your granddaughter?" And then I wanted to kick myself, because I realized that was probably the absolute wrong question to ask. But it was the only thing I knew about her, besides the fact that she had HIV or AIDS, and I sure as hell wasn't going to mention that.

Luckily, though, June didn't seem to mind the question. "She's great, thank you for asking."

I wondered if she had been allowed to hold her yet, but I didn't dare ask.

"Lucy! You came back!" Roxie's voice sing-songed from the other side of the room. She came over to where June and I were standing and handed me a mini bottle of water. I noticed that her nails were painted aqua blue today.

"Yeah," I said.

Roxie checked the time on her cell phone. It was a flip phone, like the one Dad had had when I was a little kid. I hadn't seen a phone like that in a long time—everyone I knew had smart phones now.

"All right everyone, let's get started," she called out to the room, and we found our seats. "Who would like to begin today?"

Unlike last time, no one spoke up.

"I'll go first then," she said. I found myself sitting up a little straighter in my chair, eager to hear what she was going to say.

"There was a blood drive at work on Wednesday." She gave a you-all-know-where-this-is-going smile. "The head of my department, of all people, was the one who organized it, and actually closed our office for an hour so we could all go down and donate. I felt so…so *stuck*, you know? I didn't want to look like this horrible person who was refusing to give blood for no good reason, but I didn't want to tell anyone the truth, either. I haven't been working there that long, but I know that if everyone found out, things would get real awkward real fast. And I really need this job."

"So what did you do?" someone asked.

"I ended up going down there with everyone, like everything was all good, and then pretending to get super queasy and light-headed at the sight of the blood bags. The technician was totally apologetic, but told my boss he couldn't take blood from someone in my condition. Problem solved." She grinned.

Roxie was being pretty good-natured about the whole thing, but I imagined myself in the same situation and knew it couldn't have been easy for her. I felt a stab of sympathy and then realized that someday, maybe even sometime soon, I would be faced with a predicament like that too. Maybe it would be a blood drive, or maybe it would be something else. When you had HIV, *everything* was complicated. Even a simple day at work could turn into an ordeal.

A few more people shared and then there was another stretch of silence. I could feel it coming; I didn't even have to look her way. Sure enough…

"Lucy, we'd love to get to know you a little better," Roxie said. "Do you feel comfortable sharing tonight?"

I really didn't want to talk. But all eyes were on me, and since I knew that Papa was going to keep making me come to these things, I figured I may as well spit out something now and get it over with rather than having Roxie single me out every time.

"I don't really know what to say," I admitted. "I'm new at this."

"Why don't you start with why you're here," Roxie suggested.

"I'm here because my parents are making me." That got a few laughs.

"Points for honesty," she said. "How are you feeling?"

"Right now?" I asked.

"Yeah. Right now, at this point in time, how are you feeling?"

"I'm feeling…a little cold, maybe, and sort of nervous. But other than that, totally fine." I paused briefly, thinking. "You know, that's what I'm having the hardest time with, I think. That the only reason I even know I have this disease at all is because someone told me I did. But I don't *feel* it. I feel perfectly normal. If it's really as bad as everyone says it is, shouldn't I feel something?"

"Why question it, though? Why not just be grateful that you don't feel any pain or illness?" she countered.

I shrugged. "I am grateful for that, I guess. But still, it feels wrong. I can't explain it."

"No, I get what you mean," another lady said. I thought I remembered her introducing herself as Shelly. Or was it Sally? "It's like, if you have cancer or heart disease or something, you *know* it. You probably got diagnosed in the first place because of your symptoms. But HIV is like this silent, deadly thing inside you."

"No, that's only how it is in the beginning. Just wait. It gets worse," a thin man with dry lips said.

"I know. It gets a *lot* worse," I said, remembering the photographs. "That's the point. This healthy-feeling time now just feels like a tease. Like I'm in this holding pattern, flying in smooth circles within sight of the airport, in super-comfortable first class. But I can't enjoy the in-flight movie or free chocolate chip cookies because I know that before the airport is able to make room for us, the plane is going to run out of fuel, and we're going to crash-land into a fiery, agonizing death."

The basement was completely silent.

"What?" I said.

"Wow," Shelly/Sally breathed. "That's exactly it. Are you a writer or something?"

I shook my head. "I'm an actor."

• • •

After the meeting, I met my dads outside the church.

"How'd it go?" Papa asked.

"It was okay, I guess. I 'shared' this time." I emphasized "shared" so he would know it wasn't my word.

"That's great, honey!" he said, giving me a one-armed hug as we began to walk down the street.

"We're so proud of you," Dad said, putting his arm around me too.

"Lucy!"

We all turned. Roxie was hurrying in our direction.

"Um, Dad, Papa, this is Roxie," I said awkwardly when she reached us. "Roxie runs the meeting."

I could tell they were surprised by her age, but they all shook hands and made their hellos. Roxie didn't even blink when I introduced the two men in front of her as my parents.

"You said you're an actor, right?" she asked, turning her attention back to me.

"Yeah. Why?"

"Well, I work for NYU. I'm just an admin, but if I work there for over a year I'll get free tuition. I mean, I'll have to get accepted first, and who knows if they'd even look twice at my GED, but my SAT scores are pretty good—"

"Um, Roxie?" I cut her off.

"Sorry. So they're holding auditions tomorrow for their new ad campaign. It's going to be huge—print ads, TV commercials, all kinds of fancy stuff. Mucho dinero. You're totally the look they're looking for—I know because I'm the one who's been setting up all the audition appointments. I can probably get you in if you wanna come tomorrow."

"Wow, really?" That sounded like exactly the distraction I

needed. Just the prospect of getting to act in front of people who weren't members of my own drama club had me instantly feeling more whole. "Yes, I definitely want to come."

"Hold on a second, Lu. Aren't you forgetting something?" Papa said.

Oh right. My first doctor's appointment. "Can't we reschedule?" I begged.

"Not a chance. You know what it took to get this appointment." The office had been completely booked up for the next two months, but Papa, hot-shot lawyer that he was, called in a few favors and managed to get me in for Saturday morning.

The wind left my sails. "Thanks anyway, Roxie, but I have to go to the doctor tomorrow."

"What time is your appointment?" she asked.

"Ten-thirty a.m."

"Oh, that's perfect. You can come to the audition after. I'll be there till four."

"Really?"

"Oh, totally. Give me your number, and I'll text you all the details."

We swapped phones and put our numbers into each other's contact lists.

"So, I guess I'll see you tomorrow then," I said.

"Awesome! See you tomorrow!"

22
Tear Me Down

"Fill these out," the lady behind the desk said, handing me a clip-board with about twenty double-sided pages attached to it.

My dads and I divided the forms up—they took the insurance and past medical history ones and I was left with the ones that only I could answer, like the social behaviors checklist and the descrip-tion of present condition. I took the clipboard over to a far corner of the waiting room so I could write my answers down without worrying about anyone reading over my shoulder.

When all the forms were completed, the copay had been paid, and the formalities were over, the wait began. There sure were a lot of people here for a Saturday morning on a holiday weekend. I didn't know whether to take that as a good sign or not—on one hand, it seemed this doctor was in high demand. On the other, a lot of the patients were in really bad shape. They were run-down and tired-looking, some were coughing, some were incredibly thin. Many looked utterly miserable. If this doctor was so great, why did his patients look so sick?

This was all getting way too real.

And still the wait continued. As patients were called into exam rooms, more patients came to sign in. The flow was endless. I focused on breathing and tried to ignore the queasiness in my stomach. *I'm not sick like these people,* I tried to comfort myself. *It's just nerves.*

My dads and I didn't talk much. Like magnets, our gazes kept drifting over to the muted television hanging from the ceiling, but it was nothing more than an automatic reaction to the presence of the flickering screen. I don't think any of us were really in the mood to learn about all the terrible things that were going on in the world from the CNN ticker.

Over an hour after we checked in, my name was called. My dads got up to follow me in the room, but the nurse stopped them.

"Patients only beyond this point, please."

I gave them the most reassuring smile I could, letting them know I'd be fine, even though I wasn't sure if I really would, and followed the nurse into the room. She took my blood pressure, pulse, and temperature, and then handed me a faded cotton gown. "Put this on, open to the back. You can leave your underwear on, but take off everything else, including your bra." She dropped my chart in the little plastic holder stuck to the outside of the door, and closed the door behind her.

I was all alone.

I surveyed the tiny exam room. It looked like any other doctor's office I'd ever been in. But though it was familiar, I was anything but comfortable. Shivering, I stripped down and hurriedly put the gown on, fumbling with the ties. I left my socks on. I was freezing.

I sat up on the bed, the thin paper rumpling beneath me, and covered my legs with my hoodie.

Fifteen minutes later, there was a brief knock at the door and before I could even say, "Come in," the knob turned and the doctor entered the room.

"And you are…Lucy Moore," he said, not looking up from the chart.

"Yes," I said.

He went over to the sink and washed his hands with lots of soap. "I'm Dr. Jackson." He sat down and took his time reading through all my forms. I felt entirely invisible and uncomfortably obvious all at the same time, sitting there in practically nothing in front of this stranger who was ignoring me.

Finally, he looked up. As soon as he laid eyes on my face, he frowned and flipped back through his notes, looking for something. "How old are you?"

"Seventeen," I replied.

He sighed and shook his head in clear disapproval. I'd thought doctors were supposed to be nonjudgmental.

"And how do you know you're HIV-positive, Lucy?" Dr. Jackson asked. Suddenly, his voice had taken on an entirely different tone, doing a complete one-eighty from the all-business, detached manner from when he'd first entered the room to sugary-sweet condescension.

"I was tested," I said, goose bumps erupting all over my skin, and not because of the cold.

"By whom?"

"Harlem Free Health Services."

"Where is your copy of your test results?"

"I don't have it. I got my results over the phone."

A corner of his mouth turned up in amusement. "Of course you did," he said.

What the hell was this guy's problem? He was treating me like I was a five-year-old playing dress-up.

"What grade are you in at school, Lucy?"

"Eleventh. Why?"

"Have you had sex education classes at your school?"

"Um, yeah…"

"So they've taught you all about the importance of safe sex?"

"I guess…"

"I see here that you believe you contracted HIV from engaging in unprotected sexual intercourse," he said, gesturing to the file. "That was very irresponsible behavior, Lucy."

Was he for real? He was actually *reprimanding* me?

Listen, I wanted to say. *I don't need your judgment, okay? I have enough to deal with without you contributing. So can we just get on with this so I can get out of here?*

But I couldn't form the words. Dr. Jackson viewed me as a child, and somehow, under his contemptuous gaze, I had regressed to one.

I was frightened and shy, and it was all I could do to answer his questions and count the seconds until the end of the visit.

Dr. Jackson waited for me to respond, but when I didn't he just shrugged, as if he decided I wasn't worth his little lecture. He had a whole office full of people to treat; I was just another number to him.

He stuck his head out the door and called for the nurse to join us. I felt incrementally better that I didn't have to be alone in the room with him while he was doing the physical, but I hated every second of that exam nonetheless.

He poked and prodded me all over, not even bothering to apologize for his cold hands or icy stethoscope. He had no grace whatsoever as he jammed the little light into my ears, felt for swollen glands in my neck, and pressed under my ribs to check the size of my liver and spleen.

And it got even worse, when he did the breast exam and felt for lymph nodes in my pelvic area. I did not want this man touching me in those places. It wasn't that he was being inappropriate; it was more that he obviously didn't view me as a person—let alone a scared person with actual feelings. He saw me as just another scientific specimen, there for his own experimenting. I squeezed my eyes shut, cringing the entire time.

"You can get dressed now," I heard him say. I opened my eyes to find the nurse exiting the room and Dr. Jackson back at his stool, scribbling away.

I hesitated. Wasn't he going to leave so I could dress in privacy?

Apparently not.

So I put my clothes on as quickly and discreetly as I could, facing away from him and keeping the gown on until my clothes were safely back on my body.

"All right, I'm going to send you down to the lab," Dr. Jackson said. "They will draw blood and run the CBC, T-cell subset, and RNA viral load tests. I'll need to see you back here in one week. You can make the appointment on your way out." He crossed to the door. "Any questions?"

Um, yes. What's a CBC, T-cell subset, and RNA viral load test? What did you find when you examined me? Why are you such a dick?

"No, no questions," I said.

• • •

My dads were right where I had left them. They jumped out of their seats as soon as they saw me. But I didn't go over to them.

As my physical proximity to Dr. Jackson distanced, the more my courage and anger returned. I marched straight over to the front desk, jaw clenched. My dads followed wordlessly, sensing something was up.

The lady looked up. "The doctor would like to see you back here in one week. How does next Saturday at eleven a.m. sound?"

"Horrible," I said.

Papa put a hand on my shoulder. "Lucy, I know this is hard for you—"

I spun around and glared at him. "You don't know what it was like in there. I'm never going back to that doctor again." I didn't bother to whisper; the whole waiting room was watching and listening. This must have been far more interesting than whatever was on CNN right now. I turned back to the lady behind the desk. "Do you have any other doctors here?"

She swallowed. "Yes, we have one other physician specializing in…your particular department." She whispered that last part, though I didn't really see the point. It was clear from Dr. Jackson's air of absolute boredom that people came here for one reason only.

"Who is that?" I asked.

"Dr. Vandoren."

"Yes, I'd like an appointment with him, please," I stated firmly.

"Her," the lady corrected.

"Even better," I said.

Before I could leave that god-awful medical building, I had to get my blood drawn. I watched in a trance as it was siphoned from the tiny vein in my arm, through the clear tube, into the vials. The technician repeated the process again and again, collecting eight vials in all.

When he was finally done, I moved to stand up. But the whole room went dark and spun around me like a tornado, and the next thing I knew, I was on the floor, vaguely aware of cold hands on my forehead, my eyes working to focus on the face hovering over me.

"Oh, wonderful," I said as I attempted to push myself up to sitting. "I passed out, didn't I?"

Dad nodded. "Are you okay?"

"Who even knows anymore?" I grumbled.

As the background became clearer, I realized that Papa was arguing with someone. His voice was raised, and he was gesturing wildly.

"What's going on?" I asked Dad.

"Seth is…expressing his dissatisfaction with the amount of blood they took from you."

Oh yeah, now I heard it.

"She's all of a hundred pounds!" he was shouting. "What makes you think that it's okay to take that much blood out of her?! Of *course* she's going to pass out. What kind of operation are you people running here, anyway? Don't you know how to do your jobs? I'll have you know that I am an attorney, and if there is even one bump on that child's head resulting from your negligence, I'll sue you so fast you won't even know what hit you!"

The technician's face was flushed, and he was pointing an unsteady finger toward a computer screen. "Sir, please, look. The doctor ordered eight vials. I don't make the decisions."

"Papa," I called out. "Calm down, I'm fine." I slowly stood up to prove it.

Papa exhaled when he saw me supporting myself on my own two feet, and I saw the fight leave his body. He took my hand and led us toward the elevators. "Let's get out of here," he said.

"Best idea you've had all day," I agreed.

23
Being Alive

It was two-thirty in the afternoon when we finally felt the sunshine on our faces again. We'd been in that building for over four hours.

"Why don't we go get some lunch and you can tell us what exactly happened in there," Dad said.

"I can't," I said. "I have to go to that audition."

"Lucy, please, it's been a long day, and you know how much pressure you put on yourself at auditions. Is that really what you need right now?" Papa said.

"Yes, Papa, that's exactly what I need right now." He didn't understand that performing, in any capacity, was far more therapeutic than any lame group meeting could ever be.

My dads exchanged a glance.

"Well…if you're *sure*…" Dad said.

"I am sure." I gave them each a big hug. "You guys go home. I promise I'll tell you everything later."

Five minutes later, I was on the subway, zooming downtown. The car was packed, and I had to stand near the doors. Surrounding me on three sides was a high school tourist group, all wide eyes and eager smiles, wearing matching bright orange sweatshirts that read, "I marched in the Thanksgiving Day Parade!" A guy weaved through the crowd selling self-published copies of his book of poetry. A mariachi band serenaded us all with their version of "La Cucaracha." I closed my eyes and absorbed the organized chaos of it all, letting the sounds fill up my head, so that soon there was no room left for any lingering doctor's office jitters.

I found the address Roxie had texted me easily enough.

There was only an hour left of auditions but the line was still out the door. I'd been to a few auditions in the city before, and they were always like this. Hundreds of similar-looking, similarly-dressed, non-union girls neatly lined up, shooting each other dirty looks while their own heads were filled to the brim with delusions of grandeur. I knew better. I wasn't going to get this job, just like I hadn't gotten any of the other professional roles I'd tried for in the past. It had nothing to do with talent—the competition was high and the odds were slim. The sight of so many hopeful faces was a reminder that this was a city filled with dreamers, most of whom would simply never see their dream realized.

It would have been discouraging if I was actually thinking about the job. But for the first time in my life, I wasn't focused on the end goal. All I cared about was this exact moment in time and standing in front of those casting directors, becoming a character, and leaving my own body—and everything it meant to be me—behind.

I squeezed through the crowd and made my way to the front of the line, where Roxie was sitting behind a folding table, piling up headshots and resumes and handing out numbers.

"Hey," I said.

Her face lit up. "Oh my god, yay! You made it!"

"Yeah. So, um, should I sign in or something?"

"No, that list is only for people with appointments. But don't worry, I'll get you in. Can you hang out for a while?" she asked.

"Sure." *It's not like I have any other friends to hang out with*, I thought.

"Great, just go have a seat and I'll come and get you when there's an opening."

As I maneuvered back through the crowd in search of a place to sit down, something occurred to me. My exact thought had been that I didn't have any *other* friends to hang out with. So that must have meant that somewhere, deep in my subconscious maybe, I considered Roxie to be a friend. When had that happened? I barely even knew the girl.

I found an empty patch of carpet and sat there, on the floor, for an hour. Occasionally I caught a few looks from the other girls as they eyed my outfit. I was the only one in jeans, and I barely had any makeup on. Whatever. Let them stare.

At four o'clock exactly, Roxie stood up on her chair and loudly addressed the remaining girls. "The casting team is not going to be able to see anyone else today. Sorry for any inconvenience and thanks for coming!"

An uproar of groans and complaints emerged from the crowd, and I had to stop myself from joining in. What had I waited for, then? I knew I didn't have an appointment, so I didn't have much of a right to be annoyed, but still. Roxie shouldn't have told me she could get me in if she actually couldn't.

I went back up to the sign-in table. "Well, thanks anyway," I said. "I guess I'll see you next week."

"Wait, where are you going?" she asked.

"Um, home?"

"No, silly. I told them I had a friend coming. They're expecting you."

"Oh. Really?"

"Yes!" she said. At that moment the door opened and a girl came out. "You're up!" Roxie said to me.

The room was empty, except for the two men and a woman sitting behind a desk, and a camcorder set up on a tripod. I was immediately thrust into audition mode.

"Hi," I said, a smile on my face for the first time all day. "I'm Lucy Moore." I approached the desk and forked over my headshot.

"Hello, Lucy," one of the men said, handing me a sheet of paper. "Please stand on the mark and, when you're ready, read these sides directly into the camera."

I quickly skimmed the lines. It was some boring copy about NYU being an exciting place to learn. But there was nothing exciting about the words at all. In a flash, I realized that I hadn't actually known anything about this audition. I should have asked Roxie for specifics. But I understood now that they weren't looking for an actor, they were looking for a spokesperson. A pretty face to entice people to invest four years of their lives and hundreds of thousands of dollars into an overrated education.

The smile fled from my face. I didn't want to read this. I didn't even want this job. I just wanted to get to *perform* for three lousy minutes. Was that too much to ask?

I don't remember making the decision to do it, but before I knew what I was doing, I'd tossed the paper to the floor, cleared my mind, and begun doing April's butterfly monologue from *Company*.

There may have been some murmurs of protest from the casting people, but I shut them out and continued with the little story about the cocoon and the butterfly and the cat and the boyfriend, embodying this character whose biggest problem in life is that she's a little dumb. Maybe I was losing my mind; maybe all the pressure and distress from the last two months had finally made me snap. I didn't care.

When I was finished, I refocused my attention back on the befuddled casting team.

"Well…that was…" the woman began.

Best to cut her off now, while I was still riding high. "Thank you all so much for your time," I said, and escaped from the room.

Roxie had finished packing up and was waiting for me with an eager grin. "How'd it go?"

I let out a chuckle. "Let's just say that I think they'll remember me."

"Awesome!"

I hitched my bag further up onto my shoulder. "So…thanks for this. It was really nice of you."

"No problem. We have to stick together, right?" She gave me a meaningful look.

"Oh, um, yeah, I guess."

"Wanna go grab some coffee? I don't have to be home until six."

I looked at this girl who seemed to have her life so perfectly together, who seemed so happy all the time, and I suddenly needed to know how she did it. "Okay, sure," I said.

We found a table at a little hole-in-the-wall coffee shop around the corner, and I bought us two large coffees—mine black, Roxie's filled with cream and sugar.

"I'm so glad this all worked out," she said. "I usually don't work on Saturdays but I needed the extra money."

The audition buzz was fading now, and I was starting to feel bad about what I'd done. "I kind of went off the rails in there," I confessed. "I'm so sorry—I know they only saw me as a favor to you. I hope it doesn't affect your job or anything."

"Nah, don't worry about it. I don't even work with those people. They work for the casting agency that NYU hired. I'd never even met any of them before today."

I smiled. That made me feel a lot better.

"So what did you do?" Roxie asked, a curious glint in her eye.

"I decided I'd rather do a monologue than read their dumb copy. It was actually really out-of-character for me, but after the day I've had…"

"Oh yeah, you had a doctor appointment today, right? How did it go?"

I grimaced and told her what had happened.

"Ugh! I know exactly what that's like! Some of these doctors are so arrogant, like they think that just because they're super smart they get to treat us like garbage. I've been to more of them than I can count. There was this one guy, when I was ten—"

"Wait," I cut her off. "*Ten?* How long have you had…?" It was probably too personal of a question, but I couldn't help myself.

Roxie just looked back at me, unaffected. "Since I was born."

My mouth fell open.

"My mother had it and passed it on to me," she explained.

"How old are you?"

"Nineteen."

Whoa. Nineteen years with this virus in her system. "And you're…okay?"

She shrugged. "For now. I'm on the wonder pill, and, for the most part, it's keeping the bad stuff at bay."

"For the most part?"

"I was in the hospital last year for a few weeks. Nasty bout of pneumonia."

"Do you have AIDS?" I whispered.

"Nope." She crossed her fingers. "As far as they can figure, I have at least a few more years before getting a visit from the Big Bad." She laughed.

I really didn't see what was so funny. "How can you be so cavalier about it all? Aren't you scared?"

"Of course. But I've had forever to get used to the idea. I'm not going to let it stop me from living my life."

I thought about that for a minute. "How's your mom doing?"

"Not so good. She died," Roxie said.

"Oh god, I'm so sorry."

"It's okay, it was a long time ago." She took a sip of her coffee. "It's just been my brother and me for a while now."

I felt a heart-wrenching pang. "Your brother has it too?"

She smiled and shook her head.

"But…how?"

"By the time my mom was pregnant with him, she was more educated about the whole thing. Once you're on meds, it's a lot harder to pass it on to your baby."

"Oh," was all I could say. It was beginning to dawn on me that I still had a lot to learn.

Roxie told me about growing up in foster care and being shuffled around from home to home and having to constantly fight to not be separated from her brother. The day she turned eighteen she'd filed for custody and had been working to support the two of them ever since. She'd spent most of her life in overcrowded free clinics and getting her medical care from not-for-profit organizations. It made me appreciate my own family so much more.

"Alex is the reason I work so hard at keeping myself healthy," she explained. "I don't really have the luxury of moping around feeling sorry for myself. He's only eleven—if I kick the bucket, he goes right back into the system." She paused to take a sip of coffee. "So what's *your* story?" Roxie asked.

"Me?"

"Yeah."

Crap. I *had* to tell her now, after she'd been so honest with me. So, staring into my coffee mug, I told her everything. It was easier than telling Evan and my dads—at least Roxie already knew that I had HIV.

"You've only been positive for a *month*?" Roxie said when I was finished.

"Yeah. And my dads have only known for a week."

"Oh, Lucy. How are you doing?"

"I don't know. I'm a little all over the place," I admitted.

"Well, listen, you *have* to keep coming to the meetings. Trust me, they help. I started going to them in middle school. It was nice to have a place to go where there were other people like me, you know?"

"I guess."

"Plus, I like having you there. We don't get a lot of people our age." She shrugged. "I don't really know why."

"Probably because most people our age aren't stupid enough to do what I did," I said bitterly.

"Lucy, come on. You're not stupid, you just made a mistake. It happens."

I crossed my arms and slumped down in my chair. "Some mistake."

"Well, what would *you* call it?"

"Off the top of my head? How about 'perfectly karmic punishment for the most ungrateful, spoiled brat the world has ever seen'?"

"Punishment?"

"Yes. Punishment."

"So what, you're just going to keep blaming yourself?"

"Who else do I have to blame?"

She pursed her lips. "You know, being stuck in this mindset is seriously not helping your—" *Brriiiiiinnnnggg.* Roxie's phone. "Sorry, I have to get this," she said, and flipped the phone open. "Hey, buddy…Yup, I'm on my way home right now. Tell Mrs. Wu I'll be home soon…love you too…okay, bye." She hung up and turned her attention back to me. "I have to go. I didn't realize how late it was. My brother stays with our neighbor when I'm at work, but she gets cranky when he's there all day."

"No problem," I said. I wasn't in the mood to talk anymore, anyway.

"See you Tuesday, right?" she asked.

I exhaled. "Yeah, see you Tuesday."

Roxie gathered up her stuff, took one last swig of her coffee, and dashed out the door.

It was dark out now, and I should have started making my way home too. But I couldn't stop thinking about my "mistake." My own words echoed in my head: *Who else do I have to blame?*

I would go home soon.

But there was something I had to do first.

24
Shadowland

The temperature had dropped considerably, and I was glad I'd stuffed my winter hat and gloves in my bag before I'd left the house this morning. I tugged my jacket snugly around myself as I walked.

It was only a few blocks to Spring Street, but when I reached the intersection of Spring and Mercer, I had a choice to make: right or left? Most details of that drunken night and hungover morning were still foggy in my memory and I couldn't remember the exact address, or even the cross street. All I remembered was the red door.

I took a chance and turned left, squinting through the dark and the strange glare the streetlights cast on shop windows, searching each doorway I passed. When I reached the eastern end of Spring, I knew I had chosen wrong. So I doubled back.

Fifteen minutes later, I found it.

It was smaller than I'd remembered, and the shade of red was darker and more muted than the angry burning lava it had been in my mind, but I was certain. This was Lee's apartment building. There were ten buzzers, two for each floor.

I did some quick math: I'd run down four flights of stairs that awful morning, so Lee's apartment must have been on the fifth floor. Funny, the things you remember.

The buzzers were labeled.

5A: *J. Gonzalez.*

5B: *L. Harrison.*

I closed my eyes and counted to five, my stomach doing somersaults. Then I slowly reached out and pressed 5B.

The next several seconds seemed to last an eternity, as fear hijacked my not-so-thought-out plan.

What was I doing here?

What was I going to say?

What if he didn't even remember me?

Suddenly I knew I had to get as far away from this building as possible. I shouldn't have come here. What was I *thinking*? But panic had locked my knees, and I couldn't move.

Maybe he wasn't home. That would be good.

"Hello?" a voice came through the speaker.

It was him. My mouth went dry.

"Hello?" he said again.

Don't say anything, the voice in my head commanded. *Just stay quiet, and he'll go away.*

"Um, Lee?" I heard myself say.

Lucy, you stupid, stupid girl.

"Yeah? Who's there?"

"You, um, probably don't remember me. My name is Lucy, and we, um, met a couple of months ago…"

There was a long pause. A trendy couple walked by, holding hands.

"Lucy. Right. Yeah, I remember. What are you doing here?"

"Can I come up?" I asked, not really wanting to have this conversation via building intercom.

Another unfathomably long pause.

"Now's not really a good time," he said finally.

"Just for a minute," I said. "It won't take long, I swear."

"I'm actually right in the middle of something, so…"

I knew I was supposed to get the hint, but the more he tried to get rid of me, the more I wanted in. He knew I was here to confront him about what he'd done and didn't want to face me. Well, maybe his brush-off routine had worked with people in the past, but it wasn't going to work with me. I'd come here to give Lee his share of the blame, and I wasn't leaving until I succeeded. He deserved that and so much worse.

Knowing he wasn't going to voluntarily let me in, I didn't bother replying. Let him think I'd given up and left. I adjusted my hat and scarf and huddled in the doorway, determined to wait as long as I had to.

About ten minutes later, the door opened and one of the building's residents emerged. I caught the door with my foot as it closed and slipped inside.

I dashed up the four flights quickly, trying not to think too much about what I was about to do. I would say what I came to say and get the hell out of here.

My mittened hand gave three swift strikes to Lee's door, and his muffled curses carried out into the hallway. My heart was hammering as I stood there waiting.

The door flew open, and my breath caught the moment I saw him. He was every ounce as gorgeous as he was the night we met. His shirtless torso was etched with muscles and tattoos, his skin glistening with a light sheen of sweat. His jeans were unbuttoned, like he had just pulled them up a second before. He glared at me intensely, but somehow the burning behind his eyes made his face even more radiant.

But the warm, fuzzy feelings only lasted a half-second and were immediately replaced with loathing.

I cleared my throat nervously. "I need to talk to you," I said.

He didn't say anything. Instead, he looked me up and down, the space between his eyes deeply creased.

"What?" I demanded.

"You look different," he said, confused.

I looked down at myself. In place of the skimpy black ensemble I'd been wearing last time were jeans, flats, my puffy green jacket, and rainbow-patterned wool hat and mittens. I guessed I was looking a lot more my actual age tonight.

But I was saved from having to attempt an explanation because just then I was distracted by a small movement behind Lee. There was someone else in the apartment. I shifted my position outside the door so I could see around him and managed to catch a glimpse of a woman's bare legs, partially covered by the sheets of his bed, before he swiftly stepped out into the hall and pulled the door closed behind him.

"What do you *want*?" he growled.

I stared at him, waiting for my mind to catch up to what was going on here. He hadn't been trying to avoid a confrontation—he was trying to get rid of me because he was *with* someone. A girl who surely had no idea what she was getting herself into.

I suddenly wasn't nervous anymore.

"Just how many people have you done this to?" I demanded.

"Done *what* to?"

I looked him straight in the eye. "You know what I'm talking about."

He let out a pitying little laugh. "Listen, Lucy, we had fun. But it was a one-time thing—it's not going to happen again. And I really don't have time for this right now, so you should really leave before I call the police and report you for trespassing."

Oh god—he thought I was here to have *sex* with him again? I gave him a wry smile. "Go ahead. I have a few things I'd like to report you for too."

"What the hell are you talking about?"

I sighed heavily. Might as well just say it. "You infected me."

There was a slight pause. "What do you mean, I 'infected' you?" he said, his voice less severe now. He genuinely looked baffled.

"I mean, you gave me HIV."

He barked out a laugh. "What the hell are you talking about? I don't *have* HIV."

I studied him carefully, searching for signs of lying or even guilt. But his face was smooth, his gaze steady and innocent.

This was going to be so much worse than I'd anticipated.

"Yes, you do," I said cautiously. "And you gave it to me."

Lee stared at me, his eyes wide. He shook his head. "You're wrong. You got it from someone else." But there was a trace of doubt in his words.

I watched him silently, his face twitching and jaw clenching as he worked it all out. Right now, in Lee's head, denial was warring with the undeniable facts. I knew because I'd been there. I'd felt that pull, that desperate yearning to reject what I knew was true. I wondered if my face had looked like that when Diane had told me my results.

He'd really had no idea. He'd been going around, living his life, playing his music, not having any idea that he was dying. And now here I was, the grim reaper. I wished I had never come here.

No, wait, that wasn't right. It was good that I came here. He had to know. Who knew how long he'd had it? Who knew how many people he'd passed it on to or how many people he would have in the future? Maybe I'd even saved the life of the faceless girl on the bed.

"Lee?" she called, impatient.

He and I had each been so lost in our own thoughts that the sudden draw back to the present was jarring.

We stared at each other for a tense, lingering moment.

"Lee? Are you coming back to bed?" her voice cut through again.

He blinked. "I have to go," he said and disappeared, closing the door firmly behind him.

25

With a Little Bit of Luck

I stood outside Lee's apartment door for a long time. I kept thinking that he would come back out, that after he'd had some time for everything to sink in, he would want to finish our conversation.

But he didn't.

I paced the small hallway. Maybe he and the girl were talking. Maybe she was his girlfriend, and she was comforting him as he told her what had happened. Maybe she was convincing him to come back out and talk to me.

I put my ear to the door and listened.

They weren't talking. But I did hear noises.

I gasped and backed away from the door in dismay. How could he go right back in there and continue having sex with her like nothing had even happened? There was no doubt in my mind that he'd heard—and believed—everything I'd told him. But this reaction didn't make any sense.

He was supposed to be remorseful for what he'd done to me.

He was supposed to accept the blame so that I didn't have to carry it around with me anymore. He was supposed to apologize.

I didn't understand.

Instinctively, I pulled out my phone—Max would have the answer. But halfway through dialing his number, I remembered. Max and I weren't friends anymore; I'd driven him away.

There was nothing more I could do. I only had so much energy left, and I couldn't waste it here.

So I went home, where my measly halflife awaited me.

• • •

I would never admit it to Andre, but I'd secretly become glad I hadn't been cast as Juliet. It was hard enough finding time for everything without having a whole play's worth of lines to memorize. My four little Mercutio scenes were plenty, now that I had group meetings and doctor's visits and this whole other life to contend with.

But that didn't mean I didn't want those four little scenes to be the best they could possibly be. And right now, the fight scene just wasn't cutting it.

Monday afternoon, I approached Evan at rehearsal. It was the first time I'd spoken directly to him since he'd decided he didn't want anything to do with me, but after what had happened with Lee and Dr. Jackson two days earlier, dealing with Evan suddenly ranked pretty low on my awkward encounters list.

He stood up rail-straight when he saw me headed his way and closed the graphic novel he'd been reading.

"Lucy…hi," he said.

I checked over my shoulder to make sure we were out of everyone else's earshot, and then got straight to the point. "The fight scene sucks, Evan. And I don't know how things worked back in your precious little California drama club, but this is New York. We get Broadway producers and theatrical agents at our shows, and I don't want to look like a fool up there. So you need to check your pathetic scaredy-cat *emotions* at the door, and fight me like a man. Comprende?"

He looked like a deer caught in headlights, but he managed a nod. "I'll…do my best."

"Your best better be good enough. Because this play is pretty much all I have right now, and I'm not going to let you ruin it for me."

"Yeah, okay."

Just then Andre called out to everyone from the edge of the stage. "Hello, my lovelies! Counting today we only have nine rehearsals left. Opening night is going to be here before you know it, so let's all make this time count, okay?"

"Absolutely!" Elyse said, running up the stage steps to join him. "Ty and I were *just* saying last night how we both really think this is going to be the *best* Eleanor Falls production *ever*. And as your leads, we want to thank each and every one of you for all your hard work."

At least I wasn't the only one staring at her with disdain this time. I had a feeling her condescension-veiled-in-sweetness act was beginning to wear thin on just about everybody.

I glanced at Evan. He rolled his eyes and we both laughed.

The moment was sheer miraculousness. It made me feel sort of warm—in a good way.

"So to show our thanks," Elyse continued, "we brought cookies!" She held up two tins. "Homemade chocolate chip! Now let's have a great last two weeks of rehearsal!"

Rousing cheers went up throughout the auditorium. My castmates were such a disappointment, allowing themselves to be bought so easily.

"Can you believe thi—" I began to say to Evan, but then I realized that he was no longer standing beside me and was in fact on his way up to the stage in pursuit of cookies like everyone else.

I bypassed them all and headed straight toward the prop table. Elyse could take her cookies and shove them. I wanted my sword. For some reason, I was pretty sure I would feel better once I was armed.

As I passed the cookie melee, I heard her and Ty talking.

"Aren't you going to have some, baby?" he was asking her. "Your mom worked so hard."

A-ha! Elyse didn't even make the damn cookies—her *mother* did.

"You're *not* serious," she replied. "You know I don't eat sugar!"

"Ellie, your body is perfect. You can eat whatever you want," Ty cooed.

Oh god, I literally could not listen to another word of this. I grabbed my sword, started humming "Wig in a Box" from *Hedwig* just to shut Ty and Elyse out of my head, and headed backstage.

• • •

My scene with Evan was actually going well. Probably because the animosity I was feeling after he bailed on our nice, nonhostile miracle moment in favor of Elyse's cookies added an extra layer of edginess under the lines.

Me: Tybalt, you ratcatcher, will you walk?

Evan: What wouldst thou have with me?

Me: Good King of Cats, nothing but one of your nine lives, that I mean to make bold withal, and, as you shall use me hereafter, dry-beat the rest of the eight. Will you pluck your sword out of his pilcher by the ears? Make haste, lest mine be about your ears ere it be out.

Evan: I am for you.

Ty: Gentle Mercutio, put thy rapier up.

Me: Come, sir, you passado.

Then…the fight. And it was every bit as awkward and stilted as it had been the last zillion rehearsals. From the moment we drew our swords, a shroud of hesitancy came over Evan, so thick I could almost see it. He was still afraid of me. This close to opening night, we should have been dancing—no, *flying*—fearlessly though the choreography. And instead we stumbled through it like we were blindfolded as Andre's patent sighs carried from the back of the house.

"Should we stop?" I called into the darkness.

"What would be the point? I really don't know what to do with you two anymore," Andre replied unhappily.

We were just finishing up the run-through when my phone rang.

"Sorry, I thought my ringer was off," I apologized to Ty, who was in the middle of his final monologue. Elyse shot me a malicious look from her deathbed.

I hastily located my phone and muted the ringtone. The number flashing on the screen was an unfamiliar one, but it was a 212 area code—a Manhattan number.

I ducked into the hallway and answered.

"Hello?"

"Hi, may I speak to Lucy Moore, please?" an upbeat male voice said.

"This is she."

"Lucy, this is Darren Clark from CBG Creative."

CBG Creative? Could that be…?

But why would he be calling me? There was no way I'd gotten the job.

"Hi," I said.

"I wanted to thank you for coming in on Saturday. Your audition was certainly interesting."

"Yeah, I'm really sorry about that," I said.

"Oh, it's quite all right. Now, as I'm sure you're aware, after that audition we aren't able to offer you that particular job."

"Of course. I understand." But then why was he calling me?

"That being said, we really liked you, Lucy. Your fiery

individuality was inspiring. So we had some meetings today and discussed the project with our client."

"Okay…?"

"We were all in agreement that the campaign needs more life—it was much too dry. So we've changed everything. Rather than having our spokesperson address the camera directly, as was our original plan, we want her to play several mini-roles. Costume, makeup, and locale changes, different characters—the photographer, the doctor, the politician, the violinist. And at the end of the spot, a single slogan will tie it all together: 'NYU. Be who you want to be.' What do you think?"

Why on earth would he care what *I* thought? Unless…

I gripped the phone tighter to keep it from sliding through my suddenly sweaty palm. "I think it sounds amazing."

"Good." I could hear the smile in Darren's voice. "Because you've got the job. If you're still interested, that is."

"*Are you serious?!*" I squealed. "Of course I'm still interested! Yes!"

Darren laughed. "Wonderful. We shoot mid-January. I'm going to have my assistant send you all the details. Look over the contract and let me know if you have any questions."

"I will. Thank you so, so, so much!"

"Thank *you*, Lucy. Like I said, you really were inspiring. I'm glad to have you on board. Take care and I'll be in touch." With that, he hung up.

I hugged the phone to my chest and leaned back against the wall for support. Was this really happening? Just to be sure, I checked my phone again. The CBG Creative number was right there, at the top of my incoming calls list. Proof that I hadn't imagined it. This really was happening.

I sprinted back into the auditorium, feeling more alive than I had in months. Elyse was in the middle of her death scene—I was happy it was her I got to interrupt.

"Hey, everyone!" I shouted. "I just got cast in a national television commercial!"

The entire cast and crew suddenly forgot all about Elyse and showered me with congratulations. I told them all about the project and couldn't help the twinge of pleasure I felt at their obvious jealousy.

I sought out my friends without thinking. Courtney and Evan were awkwardly hovering around the outer edges of the scene, like they didn't know how to react. Should they force themselves to join the group and celebrate along with everyone else, even though there was still a ton of personal stuff preventing that celebration from being genuine? Or should they distance themselves from the group and use this opportunity to illustrate just how not-okay things still were between us?

I was watching them watching me when Max's smiling face popped up in my line of vision. "Congrats, Lucy," he said.

He called me Lucy, not Luce like he always used to, and he didn't say anything more, but what with the way Courtney and Evan were acting, Max's simple "congrats" felt like an enormous gift.

I smiled back. "Thanks," I said, glowing with happiness. Maybe this tiny exchange was just what we'd needed—the first step on the road to repairing our friendship.

Suddenly, Ty pushed through the crowd and pulled me into a giant embrace, lifting me up off the ground. "I am so proud of you, Lu," he whispered. I melted into his warmth, his strength. God, I had missed this.

Elyse hadn't moved from her spot on the stage. Still in Ty's arms, I flashed her a smug grin. Her glare burned right back.

26
You've Got to Be Carefully Taught

Dad lifted his ginger ale. "To Lucy. May this only be the first in a lifetime filled with successes!"

"To Lucy!" Papa echoed.

"Isn't it bad luck to toast with a nonalcoholic beverage?" Lisa grumbled.

Dad gave her a look. "We're not a very superstitious household."

She just rolled her eyes and helped herself to a sizeable piece of lasagna.

For the first time in ages, the four of us were having dinner together. There were no meetings or appointments of any kind tonight, and both my parents had come home from work early when they heard my big news. Lisa had been on her way out the door when Dad stopped her. I was in the next room and overheard their conversation, which went something like this:

Dad: Where are you going?
Lisa: Like you care.

Dad: Well, Lucy just got some great news and we're going to have a little celebratory dinner tonight. We'd like you to join us.

Lisa: Sorry, I have plans.

Dad: Sorry, but that wasn't a request.

End scene.

Now, as she shoved garlic bread in her mouth, I realized I hadn't seen much of Lisa lately. The first couple of months she'd been with us, she had always been around, lounging on the couch or rummaging through the fridge or asking for rides. But the past few weeks she'd been a ghost. I wondered what that was all about. I didn't think she knew anyone in Eleanor Falls.

But I just shrugged it off and dug into my meal. Today was the first truly good day in a long time, and I wasn't going to taint it by worrying about Lisa.

"So what did you think of the contract, Papa?" I asked between bites.

"It looks pretty standard," he replied, nodding his approval. "Union pay scale and residuals, and full compliance with child labor laws. Pursuant to New York State law, a percentage of your earnings will be sent to a trust fund that you'll be able to access when you become of age. Hmm…I could probably negotiate free tuition to NYU too."

I sighed. College wasn't big on my list of priorities lately. "Maybe," I said.

"What do you mean, maybe?" he said, frowning. "You do still want to apply there, right? With your grades—"

Dad cleared his throat loudly.

"Right. A conversation for another time," Papa said. "Anyway, yes, it is a good contract."

"And such a great opportunity for you, honey!" Dad chimed in. "I bet you're glad you met Roxie when you did."

"Who's Roxie?" Lisa asked.

Roxie! I'd totally forgotten to call her!

"I have to go make a phone call," I said. "Thanks for dinner. It was delicious."

I ran up to my room and grabbed my phone, surprised to see I had an unread text message from Ty.

So proud of you! ☺

I smiled, texted back a quick Thanks!!! ☺, and dialed Roxie's number. She answered on the fourth ring.

"Lucy?"

"I got the job!" I said.

"What job? Wait—*the* job?"

"Yes! And they're going to change it, so I actually get to act and play all different characters. It's going to be awesome."

Roxie's screams pierced my eardrum. "Oh my god, that's *amazing*! You're gonna be famous!"

I laughed. "Well, I don't know about *that*, but it's a pretty good start, I think."

"Okay, we totally have to celebrate. How about dinner before the meeting tomorrow night? Your treat."

I laughed again. "Well, I have rehearsal until five-thirty, so the earliest I could get down there would be six or six-thirty. Would that be okay?"

"Totally. I know a great Indian place in the East Village. It's totally cheap, and they give you free ice cream."

"Sounds perfect."

• • •

The Indian place was the craziest restaurant I'd ever seen. It was about the size of my bedroom, and there were a total of five tables in the entire restaurant. Funky disco-Indian music was playing, and the walls and ceiling were absolutely covered in twinkling Christmas lights, some draped so low they were grazing the tops of our heads. In the center of the room, a disco ball was hung, even though there was barely enough room between tables to walk, let alone dance.

"The best part about this place is that it's BYOB," Roxie was saying, as she withdrew a bottle of champagne from her purse.

"Oh, I don't know…" I said. I wasn't quite sure I was ready to get back on the drinking horse, after what had happened last time.

"Just one glass," Roxie promised. "It's the only way to properly celebrate."

"Okay. Just one glass."

We clinked glasses and sipped our champagne. The bubbles went right up my nose, and I sneezed.

"Gesundheit!"

"Danke," I replied, giggling.

We ordered samosas, chana saag, and chicken tikka masala, and the food came almost immediately. We ate and drank, and talked and laughed, and soon I felt like I had known Roxie my whole life. Maybe it was the almost sisterly connection I felt with her, or maybe it was just the champagne going to my head, but I suddenly wanted to ask her things. I had so many questions, and something told me that Roxie was going to be more informative than any doctor or website would ever be.

"If I asked you some questions," I said, "would you answer them honestly?"

"Honey, I am an open book," she said, smiling.

I took another swig of champagne and nodded. "Who knows you have HIV?"

"My brother, Mrs. Wu, my doctors, my friend Monica, and everyone at the meetings," she answered without missing a beat.

"Nobody at work knows?"

"Nope."

"What about when you were in school? Did you tell anyone there?"

"No way, José."

"Why not?"

"My doctors told me not to. It causes all sorts of problems—parents not wanting their kids to be on sports teams with you, teachers giving you pity grades, everyone always looking at you like you've got three boobs. I've seen it happen—it's not pretty."

"How is it that you've been positive for nineteen years without getting AIDS?"

"Meds, baby." She took a huge bite of samosa.

Hmmm. The websites I'd looked at didn't mention that medication could do that.

"Have you ever gotten one of those lesions?" I asked.

"Not the purple ones, but I've had thrush."

"What's that?"

"This gross white rash in your mouth. It's nasty," Roxie said matter-of-factly.

I swallowed. Okay, new subject. "Have you ever had a boyfriend?"

"Yeah, of course."

"Have you had sex with them?"

"Duh."

My eyes widened. "But how?"

"Condoms, female condoms, flavored condoms, dental dams…"

"Okay, okay. But aren't you scared of something going wrong and accidentally passing it on to someone else?"

"Yeah, sometimes. But what are you going to do, never have sex again? How realistic is that?"

"I don't know…"

"And besides, it's pretty difficult for a girl to give it to a guy during sex. Not impossible, but difficult. And that's if you don't use anything. So if you use protection, you should be in the clear."

I mulled that over for a minute. "What about having a baby?"

"What about it?"

"Well, I know you said that if you're on meds it's possible to have a baby without passing on the HIV, but what about getting pregnant in the first place? How do you do that if you're supposed to use a condom every time you have sex?"

"Ever hear of artificial insemination?" Roxie said.

I sighed. "That's not very romantic."

"Oh believe me, there's *nothing* romantic about this disease. Every single thing about it totally blows." She looked me in the eye. "But you get used to it."

"I don't think I'll ever get used to it," I admitted.

"You will because you have to." She paused and studied me. "You really don't know much about any of this, do you?"

"Well, I went online—"

"*Never* go online looking for medical information." She looked horrified. "Half of the stuff on the Internet is completely inaccurate and the other half is taken out of context. It's a disaster."

"Really?"

"Really." She dug around in her oversized bag and came up with a few items. "Here," she said, sliding the books and pamphlets across the table at me. "These are really good. And I have some more books at home that I'll bring you."

I read the titles. *New York State's HIV/AIDS Laws and Regulations. HIV and You: Living Your Best Life. 101 Facts about HIV and AIDS.*

"You carry these around with you all the time?" I asked, raising an eyebrow.

"Occupational hazard," Roxie replied with a shrug.

The waiter placed our free ice cream in front of us, bringing me back to the room. As Roxie checked her phone, I realized we'd consumed all the food plus the entire bottle of champagne.

"We gotta go," Roxie said. "Meeting starts in ten."

We scarfed down our dessert and ran across town, the champagne keeping us warm on this freezing November night.

• • •

An hour later, my buzz had faded. Several people had already shared, including Ahmed and Sally/Shelly. The warm basement and the constant lull of voices were making it really hard to keep my eyelids from drooping.

But then I heard my name, and I was at full attention.

"Lucy," Roxie said, "we haven't heard from you yet tonight."

I gave her a look that I hoped said, *Yeah, you have. At dinner, remember? Now leave me alone and go pick on somebody else.*

But apparently my message didn't get through.

"I remember you saying you felt like you deserved to be punished for your choices. Do you still feel that way?" she said.

I gave her the death stare. "I guess."

"Why?" she pressed.

"I don't know."

"Well, maybe we can help you better understand what you're feeling. Why don't you share your story with the group?"

"What story?"

"The events in your life that led to you becoming HIV positive."

I glanced around the circle at all the attentive, listening faces. Roxie already knew my story. Why was she putting me on the spot like this? "I don't know…" I said, unsure.

"Lucy, each of us here has shared our own story at some point with the group. It's an important part of the process. Isn't that true?" she asked of the room. Every single person nodded their emphatic agreement.

Well, maybe it had worked for them, but it wasn't going to work for me. I wasn't like them. I didn't tell strangers my personal business. And, despite having been forced to listen to the altogether dreary details of their daily lives for the past few meetings, that's what they were. Strangers.

And they were all *staring* at me. Roxie, June, Ahmed, Sally/Shelly, the guy in the wheelchair, the lady with the mole above her right eyebrow, the woman who always showed up in her security guard uniform.

I looked at Roxie. "I really don't see how it would help anything…"

"Lucy," Roxie said, urging me on with her gaze. "Trust me."

I really didn't want to do this, but I was trapped. Resentfully, I cracked my knuckles, took a deep breath, and began. "I met this guy in a club—"

"No," Roxie interrupted. "Start at the *very* beginning."

"The very beginning?"

"Yup."

"Fine," I relented. "But when you're all dying of boredom, don't say I didn't warn you." Too late, I realized my word choice. "I mean…not *dying*…umm…you know what I mean…" My face was getting hot.

Roxie smiled. "Lucy, stop stalling."

What did she know? I wasn't stalling.

Okay, maybe I was stalling a little bit.

But there was still more than a half hour left in the meeting, and I was going to have to begin sooner or later.

"Well, I was really upset because things kept going wrong…" I started. I told them all about the play and Elyse and Ty, and when I got to the part about Lisa, there were some actual gasps from several group members. Their reaction made me think that maybe I hadn't been being overly dramatic—maybe all of this crap in my life actually *was* a big deal.

Encouraged, I continued with the story, feeding on the nods of understanding and head shakes of sympathy.

When I'd exhausted every last detail I could think of, I said, "So that's pretty much it. That's how I ended up here."

To my amazement, the group actually *applauded*. I couldn't stop the little smile that crept up onto my face. An actor does love her applause.

"Well done," Roxie said, grinning.

Phew. I'd shared, and it hadn't been horrible. I actually felt *better* somehow. Maybe Roxie really did know what she was doing with these meetings.

"Now," she said, addressing the group, "does anyone have any insight into Lucy's story?"

A few hands went up.

My heart stopped. Wait a second—people were going to *talk about* what I'd just told them? I thought the whole point was just to share and move on. We never analyzed anything anyone else said. This wasn't fair!

"Hold on," I said, panicking. "I don't really feel the need for comments. Why don't we just let someone else share?"

"Our job here is to help each other, Lucy. You were really courageous in sharing your journey with us, but it's clear you're still stuck in your own head, and that you're still holding on to a lot of self-blame. I think it will help you to get the perspectives of others."

"But…" I protested meekly.

Roxie ignored me and began calling on people to share their unwelcome opinions on my life. I sat there in horror as one by one, they weighed in.

"You know, Lucy, what you told us about your friends—Max and Cassie?" Ahmed began.

"Courtney," I mumbled.

"Right. Well, something just like that happened to me too when

I started taking better care of myself. I stopped drinking and going out all the time, and I started coming to these meetings, and all of a sudden my friends didn't want to be friends anymore. They said I thought I was too good for them." Ahmed hung his head sadly. "I haven't seen them in years."

Some other people chimed in then, saying that they'd also lost friendships because of their positive status.

And this was somehow supposed to make me feel *better*?

The security guard lady was talking now. "I think it was crazy brave of you to go confront that musician douchebag." She leaned across a few people to give me a high five. I returned it halfheartedly.

People kept talking and talking, not having any idea that this was all completely useless. Everything they said was wrong. It wasn't *bravery* that had brought me to Lee's; it was temporary insanity. And Ahmed's nameless, faceless, alcoholic friends were nothing compared with what Max and Courtney and I had had—and lost.

Roxie was wrong. This wasn't helping me at all. It only proved that even after I poured my heart out and told them the most private details of my life, these people still knew nothing about me.

And honestly, hearing it repeated over and over again that broken and abandoned relationships were not rare in the HIV/AIDS community just made me even more depressed.

There were only a few minutes to go before the end of the meeting, and I was itching to get the hell out of there. I was never going to forgive Roxie for this. I couldn't believe I trusted her, that

I actually thought she was my friend. She may have done a nice thing by getting me that audition, but this little stunt just overshadowed any kindness she'd shown me in the past.

The comment session was winding down when June raised her hand. I cursed under my breath. She was the only one who hadn't yet seized on the opportunity to pick apart my life, and I'd been hoping it would stay that way.

"Go ahead, June," Roxie said.

No, June, don't go ahead. Keep your mouth shut, so we can all go home.

"I wanted to say something about Lucy's mother," she said.

Wonderful. I was in for yet another tirade on how absolutely awful neglectful parenting and matriarchal abandonment was. I got it, ditching your kid to go take pictures and do drugs was bad.

"I was thinking about what Roxie said about how you blame yourself, Lucy, and how you feel like getting HIV was a kind of penance for your actions. Well, I think you shouldn't blame yourself at all."

Thanks, June. That's really helpful.

"It seems to me that, when all those things were happening to make you upset, you did exactly what you were supposed to do."

Huh. That was interesting. My ears perked up.

"What do you mean?" I asked.

"Look at your mother. She had you and then ran away. She came to visit you as a child and when things got too serious, she ran away again. And where did she go each time? To travel the world with musicians. You said she told you that she's had a few abortions, right? And now she's pregnant again and without a partner? So presumably she's been out there engaging in irresponsible sex."

"That's true," I said, "but what does that have to do with me?"

"Don't you see? Running away from difficult situations and landing in the bed of a stranger—a musician in particular—was learned behavior. That's what you were *taught*. You can't blame yourself for what you did, Lucy. But you can blame your mother."

Whoa.

• • •

The meeting finally ended, and Roxie threw her arms around me. "That was *so* great, Lucy. How do you feel?"

I pulled away and wedged several inches of space between us. "I don't know—I need time to process. But that wasn't cool, Roxie."

She frowned. "What wasn't cool?"

"Putting me on the spot like that."

"But it helped. I know it did!" she insisted.

"Listen to what I'm saying to you! I told you all that stuff in confidence and then you just went and threw it all right back in my face, in front of everyone. You *ambushed* me."

"I was just trying to help…"

I sighed. "I'm sure you were. But it made me really uncomfortable and right now I just need to be alone. I'll see you Thursday."

I left her standing there in the church basement, frozen in place, and, for once, speechless.

27
Louder Than Words

I didn't cross paths with Lisa until the following evening. She was rummaging through the fridge, her ever-expanding butt floating out behind her, when I got home from rehearsal.

She didn't appear to have heard me come in, and my first instinct was to creep by her and sneak up to my room unnoticed. But something stopped me, and instead I planted myself in a kitchen chair and observed her, the gestating exotic creature scavenging for sustenance.

I hadn't been able to stop thinking about what June had said. Could she have been right? Could I have been subconsciously brainwashed to copy Lisa's behavior? I'd always prided myself on being independent. I had two amazing parents and everything I ever could have needed; this wasn't a case of feeling unloved or having had some sort of neglected childhood. I hadn't had anything close to what Roxie had had to grow up with.

But what if Lisa's very existence had corrupted me, worked its way inside me when I was just a little kid, and pushed me in Lee's direction? That would mean this living hell I'd fallen into *wasn't* entirely my fault. Some of it—even just a small piece—was Lisa's. Maybe, if I'd never known her, I wouldn't have even *thought* to go home with Lee. Maybe, if she had simply handed me over to Dad after I was born and then stayed away, I wouldn't be in this situation now.

She finally finished fishing around in the fridge and kicked the door closed. But when she turned and saw me sitting there, silently glowering at her, she yelped and lost her grip on her armful of sandwich fixings.

"Christ, Lucy, you scared me," she said, squatting down to collect the food. I didn't get up to help her.

"Sorry," I said, making it absolutely clear that I was not even a little bit sorry.

She gave me a weird look but continued her sandwich-making mission. Clearly, it was going to take a lot more than a sarcastic attitude to come between a pregnant freeloader and her pile of free food.

"Why did you come back?" I demanded.

Lisa paused for an instant so quick it was almost nonexistent and then resumed slathering two pieces of bread with mayonnaise. "I already told you," she said.

"No, not this time. I mean, why did you come back those times when I was little?"

That got her to finally put the food down. "Because I wanted to see you."

The carefully arranged mask of innocence on her face caused something to snap inside me.

"Don't lie to me!" I screamed, and pounded my fists on the table. Lisa sucked in her breath and her eyes grew huge.

"I'm not," she said unconvincingly.

"You think I don't remember? The first time you came back you were so strung out you couldn't even look at me. That's not a mother who wants to see her daughter. You were here because you needed money, and you knew Dad would give it to you."

She narrowed her eyes at me. "But what about the second time? I didn't ask for money then," she said indignantly. At least she didn't bother denying my accusation. We both knew it was the truth.

"The second time was even worse! At least when you were all drugged up, I knew you weren't worth my time. But the second time, you actually pretended to *care* about me!" Angry tears were starting to come now, but I didn't wipe them away. "I didn't need you, Lisa. I was doing perfectly fine without you. So why did you come back?"

She lowered her gaze. "Because I wanted to see how you were doing. It's the truth, Lucy. I missed you."

"You missed me," I repeated, not believing her for a second. "So you decided the best thing for the thirteen-year-old daughter that you *missed* so much would be to come put on a big motherly show, make me love you, and then take it all away without so much as a good-bye? Oh yeah, that's someone who cares about her kid."

"What do you want me to say?" Lisa shouted back. "I'm messed up. That's my only excuse."

"Are you kidding me? That's not an excuse at all! You're *messed up* because you chose to be. No one forced those drugs into your veins or up your nose or whatever it is that you do. No one made you leave your family. You did all that. The only person you care about is yourself."

Her hand flew to her stomach. "That's not true."

"Oh, that's right," I said, letting out a humorless laugh. "The baby that you actually *do* want. Because, somehow, that kid is going to make you into a decent person. You know, I feel really bad for that baby. It's not even born yet, and it's already expected to do the impossible." I shook my head. "Do you have any idea how much you've managed to screw me up, Lisa? I actually *have* a family, people who love me unconditionally, and you've been in my life all of a collective five minutes. Yet somehow your toxicity managed to cut through it all and damage me in ways you couldn't possibly imagine. So yeah, good luck, little unborn baby. With a mother like this, who needs enemies?"

I stormed out of the kitchen.

• • •

I slammed my door, threw my earphones on, and blasted my iPod. I hated her. I didn't care about the baby anymore—I just wanted that woman out of my house and out of my *life* once and for all.

I lay on my bed, still fuming, and stared vacantly at the ceiling for a long time.

But one *Wicked*, one *Legally Blonde: The Musical*, and half a *Ragtime* cast album later, I heard a noise downstairs. I quickly turned the volume down on "Wheels of a Dream" and listened. My dads were home, and there was a lot of indecipherable yelling layered on top of the sounds of feet pounding as they moved around frantically. I could also hear Lisa, but she wasn't yelling so much as moaning. In pain? Despair? I strained to hear but couldn't make out any words. What the hell was going on down there?

Unable to just listen any longer, I ran downstairs and gasped at the sight before me.

Lisa was balled up on the floor of the guest room, clutching her stomach and screaming in agony. There was blood covering her lower half and slowly spreading onto the carpet beneath her. Papa was on the phone, pacing the room and trying to explain what was happening to, I assumed, a 911 operator, his face panic-stricken. Dad was kneeling beside Lisa, futilely trying to get her to stop wailing long enough to tell him what had happened.

I was frozen in place.

Did I do this?

Did my attack on Lisa send her pregnancy into distress?

My offhand thoughts about not caring about the baby came rushing back to me.

"I didn't mean it!" I cried. "I'm sorry!"

Suddenly, I was out of my body. The scene became muted and I felt like I was watching everything through a scrim. My feet stayed on the floor, but my spirit lifted up and floated over the room.

Dad hung up the phone and said something to me. But he said it to my body. My detached spirit didn't hear. He rattled my shoulders, trying to get a reaction. Unsatisfied, he ran out of the room in the direction of the front door. The ambulance must have been here.

A moment later, two men in EMT uniforms rushed in and pushed past my hollow body. One tended to Lisa, taking her pulse and listening to her stomach with a stethoscope. The other turned his attention to Dad and Papa, trying to get answers. Dad and Papa responded, gesturing wildly. But to spirit-me, everything lingered in perfect silence. The men lifted Lisa onto a stretcher and took her away. Dad and Papa followed close behind, their clothes stained with Lisa's blood.

I remained suspended above the now-still room.

But then my gaze landed on something, and I was violently sucked back into my body. I pried my feet off the ground and ran over to Lisa's bedside table, which Dad and Papa must not have noticed in the commotion.

Laid out on the table was an open, near-empty bag of cocaine.

28

Two Lost Souls

"Miss Williams has suffered what is called a placental abruption," the doctor explained.

I'd shoved the cocaine baggie into a Ziploc and followed my dads to the hospital. When I found them in the emergency room waiting room, I showed them what I'd found, and Papa informed the medical staff. The three of us sat, shell-shocked, in the waiting room for several hours, not being told anything about Lisa's status.

But now, finally, we were getting some information.

"What is that?" Dad asked.

"It's when the placenta, which is the organ that provides nourishment to the fetus, detaches from the uterine wall. It's rare to see in healthy pregnancies; however, the use of cocaine during pregnancy does greatly increase the chances of it happening."

Dad rubbed his temples. "Is the baby okay? Is Lisa okay?"

The doctor nodded. "There was only a partial uterine separation, so we were not forced to do an emergency C-section.

Because Miss Williams is just now entering her third trimester, the chance of birth defects would have been very high should we have had to deliver. But we were able to stabilize both mother and fetus through blood transfusions and the administering of IV fluids." He paused to give us each a meaningful look. "They were very lucky."

Dad shook the doctor's hand. "Thank you so much. We appreciate everything you've done to help them both."

"A word of advice—keep an eye on her. It is absolutely crucial that she not engage in any more illicit drug use during this pregnancy. Consider today a wakeup call," he said sternly.

"We will," Dad said, nodding profusely. "When can we take her home?"

"I want to keep her here for a few days to monitor her for shock and the fetus for any signs of distress. If all goes well, I would say she can probably go home this weekend."

They were still running some tests on Lisa, so we had to wait awhile longer before we could see her. We returned to our seats in the waiting room. It was already after midnight, but I don't think any of us were very tired.

We sat there in silence for a long while, half watching a *Seinfeld* rerun on the waiting room's fuzzy TV.

My phone buzzed.

Any more news on the commercial? When do you shoot?

I turned the phone off. I couldn't think about Ty or the

commercial right now; there was something I needed to confess. "It was my fault," I said into the quiet.

"What was your fault, honey?" Papa asked.

"Lisa taking the drugs. I confronted her today. I pretty much screamed in her face, blaming her for everything and telling her what a terrible mother she is going to be to the new baby." I took a deep breath. "That's why she did the drugs. It was because of what I said."

Papa opened his mouth to respond but I kept talking.

"And I should have named the baby." I was suddenly feeling guilty about that too.

"What do you mean?" Papa said.

"Lisa asked me to name the baby. Maybe if I'd done that, she would have felt like I cared more and wouldn't have gone and done this."

Dad and Papa looked at each other.

"Lucy," Dad said, "Lisa took the drugs because she has a problem. It wasn't your fault."

"Whatever," I mumbled. I knew the truth.

A short time later, a nurse told us we could go in and see her. She was propped up in the hospital bed, a white blanket covering her large belly, hooked up to all kinds of monitors and IVs.

I don't think my dads knew what to say any better than I did. The air was thick. I stayed close to the door, not saying much of anything. I'd said enough today.

"How are you feeling?" Dad asked.

"Better. The pain is gone," she said.

"That's good."

Then Papa spoke up. "Lisa, you have to be honest with us. I thought the whole point of you staying with us during the pregnancy was because you wanted to stay healthy. What the hell happened?"

"I do want to stay healthy," Lisa insisted. "But it's hard."

"That's not an explanation," Papa said.

Lisa shrugged.

"Where did you get the cocaine?" Papa asked.

"From Serge."

"Serge? Who the hell is Serge?"

"He's a guy I met a couple months ago."

"You're not telling me you've been doing drugs for a couple of months…?"

"Like you care!" Lisa said.

"Lisa," Dad stepped in, clearly trying to set an example with his calm voice, "of course we care."

"Could have fooled me. No one has even looked at me twice in the last two months. The two of you are so bloody consumed with Lucy all the time. 'Why is Lucy so down in the dumps?'" she said in a terrible American accent, mocking my dads. "'Oh gee, I hope Lucy's okay.' 'Let's have our little secret family meetings with Lucy and not invite Lisa to any of them.' 'We're going to the city with Lucy, Lisa. You can fend for yourself for dinner.'"

We stared at her in shock.

"I swear, I don't even know why you had me come to live with you in the first place. At least Serge understands me." She crossed her arms firmly over her expanded middle, sulking.

Papa was at her bedside in two broad strides. He put his face close to hers and spoke fiercely. "You want our attention? You got it. For the next three months you will be watched like a hawk. You will not go anywhere near so much as an aspirin until that baby is born, do you understand me? And once the baby is out, so are you. You will never be welcome in our home again."

Papa stormed out of the hospital room, and Dad and I followed wordlessly, too stunned to do anything else.

"Lucy, I hope you see now that none of this was even remotely your fault. That vile woman is a lost cause," Papa growled as we fled the scene.

We exited the hospital to find that it had begun to snow.

29
Maybe This Time

Heavy snow canceled school Thursday and Friday. That meant rehearsals too. It wasn't the best timing, what with the show set to open in a week, but it was just as well, because after what had happened with Lisa, I hadn't been sleeping very well and I was grateful to have time to recuperate.

I had the house all to myself. We were rid of Lisa for at least three days, and Dad and Papa still had to go to work.

Friday afternoon, I made myself some soup for lunch and watched the snow falling from the living room picture window. Everything was so still, so beautiful. It was hard to imagine that this was the same world where so many people were dying senselessly, where pregnant women were willing to put their babies' lives in danger, where fear triumphed over love.

Gazing out at the white-blanketed front lawn, I was transported back to a time where everything was so much simpler. There were Courtney, Max, and I, bundled up in snowsuits and hats and boots, building a snowman on the front lawn. We outfitted him with a feather boa and a cardboard Happy Birthday hat, and used walnuts for his eyes and nose and a piece of licorice for his mouth. We called him Jonathan. Courtney proclaimed he was a prince and that we should build him a princess, so they could be married. But Max and I had a better idea…we built another snowman, gave him a belt and a backpack, and called him Andrew. When we were finished, we stood back to admire our work—Eleanor Falls's first gay snow-couple—and collapsed in a giggling heap into a snow bank.

But now, under the luminescent gloss that the snow had painted onto the world, I had never felt so alone.

• • •

I was just settling down on the couch to watch a movie when I heard the unmistakable crunch of tires on packed snow crawling up the driveway.

Who could that be? I knew it wasn't Dad or Papa, and after my disagreement with Roxie the other night, I officially had zero friends.

I opened the front door, squinting into the falling snow, shivering against the cold.

I knew that car. It was Ty.

He trudged up the unshoveled walk, grinning. "Hey, Lu," he said.

"What are you doing here?"

He held up a paper bag. "I brought you hot chocolate."

I couldn't deny the little skip my heart did when I saw him. No matter what had happened in the past, Ty on my doorstep was a welcome sight. But still, I was suspicious. "Why?" I asked.

"Because it's a snow day and we always spend snow days together."

"And?"

"And I've been thinking about you a lot lately."

"And?"

"And I really miss you."

I searched his face, my pulse racing with possibility. His expression was open, genuine. Ty missed me.

I opened the door wider, and he came inside.

• • •

In times past, Ty and I would have been cuddled up together on the couch, under a blanket, intertwined so that our legs and arms were indistinguishable from one another's. As it was now, we were sitting on not quite opposite ends of the couch, but definitely with enough space between us to make the distance feel awkward. I flipped through the movie channels, looking for something to put on.

"What do you feel like watching?"

"I'm actually not really in the mood to watch anything," he said.

I glanced at him. "What are you in the mood for—"

But I cut myself off. Ty was staring at me, a dazzling grin fixed on his lips.

Transfixed, I switched the TV off and slowly slid closer to him. He placed his hand on my cheek and tenderly touched his lips to mine. My skin was instantly on fire. It felt like my entire body had been charged with defibrillator paddles.

The kiss became more passionate, but after a moment, I pulled back. "Wait. What about Elyse?"

He shook his head. "It's not working with Elyse. I made a mistake."

Relief flooded through me, and I kissed him again, even more intensely. Soon we were all over each other, horizontal on the couch.

As we kissed and ran our hands all over each other, my mind was reeling with contradictions.

The rational half of me was broadcasting, in flashing, neon lights: *Don't do this.*

I should stop to remember how badly Ty had treated me in the past. I should consider whether I even felt the same way about him anymore. I should think about my feelings for Evan.

And, for the love of all things holy, before we went any further, I should tell him about the HIV. That was the right thing to do.

But the rational half of me was beaten down into oblivion by the irrational half.

Roxie had said that as long as I used a condom, it was next to impossible to pass the HIV on. She knew what she was talking about—she'd had HIV for nineteen years. If she could have sex, so could I, dammit!

I didn't want to be alone anymore. And here was this hot guy, who meant so much to me, telling me he wanted me. There was no way I was going to say no to that. Not when I needed him the most.

• • •

When it was over, we lay together, skin-to-skin, under the blanket. I closed my eyes as he stroked my hair, and breathed him in.

"I missed you," I whispered.

"Me too," he said. There was a long, peaceful moment of quiet. "By the way, congratulations again on getting the commercial. That's amazing."

I smiled. "Thank you."

"It's national, right?"

"Yup."

"Do you think there's any chance you could get them to find a part for me?" he asked.

I lifted my head up to look at his face. "In the commercial?"

"Yeah."

"Oh, um…I don't think there are any other parts. I think it's just going to be me."

Disappointment appeared and then vanished on his face so quickly I thought I'd imagined it. "Oh, right. It was just a thought."

I put my head back down on his chest.

"I bet you're gonna be able to sign with a major agent after this," he said.

I shrugged. "I don't know, maybe."

"Oh, you totally will. And then you could refer me, and we could both be repped by the same agency. Think how awesome it would be, the two of us living in the city and going on auditions together, just like we've always talked about. Maybe we could even move to L.A.!"

Now I was the one who was frowning. We *had* always talked about living together after I finished high school, but for some reason I didn't want to talk about it right now. I sat up and began pulling on my clothes. "You hungry?" I asked, ready to change the subject.

Ty started getting dressed too. "Nah, I'm good." He looked at the clock. "Actually, I should go, before your dads get home."

A lump began to form in my throat. My dads had never minded Ty being over before, and he knew that.

"Okay, sure," I said, fighting to keep my expression emotionless.

He gave me a quick kiss and headed for the door. "This was amazing," he said, turning back momentarily. "I mean, how awesome are snow days?" He grinned.

I nodded weakly. "Yeah. Totally awesome."

And then he vanished into the blizzard.

30
A Fact Can Be a Beautiful Thing

My dads had let the Thursday and Friday group meetings slide because of the snowstorm, but they ardently refused to let me bail on Saturday's doctor appointment.

We took the train into the city because the roads were still a mess, and cabbed it across town from Grand Central to the medical center. The closer we got to the building, the more the butterflies in my stomach seemed to multiply.

"It's going to be okay, Lucy," Dad said, noticing my white knuckles clenched nervously around the shoulder strap of my bag. "Remember, you're going to a different doctor this time."

"I'm sure she'll be better," Papa said. "And if not, we'll keep searching until we find the doctor that's right for you, I promise." Papa still felt bad about the Dr. Jackson debacle.

Even though it was the same practice, the lady at the front desk made us refill out the paperwork. Apparently Dr. Vandoren had a different record-keeping system than Dr. Jackson. It was like some cruel déjà vu.

As I waited for my name to be called, my mind kept wandering back to Ty. He hadn't called or texted me since he left the house yesterday. I checked my phone about once every twenty seconds, but it remained silent. Where was he? Wasn't he thinking about me as much as I was thinking about him?

"Expecting a call?" Papa eyed me curiously.

I shoved the phone back in my bag. "No."

Not expecting, just hoping, I thought.

Just then, I heard my name. A different nurse from last time escorted me through a different door. She led me down a short hallway and gestured to an open door.

"Have a seat. The doctor will be with you shortly," she said.

It wasn't an exam room—it was Dr. Vandoren's office. There was a big wooden desk with papers and files stacked all over it, bookshelves with numerous medical books, and framed photos of her family everywhere. There was also a shelf with several thank-you notes propped up on it. I couldn't see inside any of them, but I was curious. Could they have been from patients? I was debating sneaking a peek at one when the doctor breezed through the door.

"Hello, Lucy," she said, and sat down behind the desk. "I'm Dr. Vandoren."

She was in her early fifties, with shoulder-length dark hair peppered with eccentric streaks of gray. She wore blue-framed glasses and had a red ribbon pinned to her white coat. Most importantly, though, she was looking at me, wearing an inviting smile. I already liked her heaps better than Dr. Jackson.

"Hi," I said shyly.

"I understand you saw Dr. Jackson last week?"

"Yeah."

"What made you request an appointment with me then, may I ask?"

How was I supposed to explain? I couldn't very well tell her how revolted I was by the man. They were probably friends. "I…wasn't exactly…comfortable with him," I said.

Dr. Vandoren smiled and nodded understandingly. "Yes, he's not known for his bedside manner."

"That's an understatement," I muttered.

To my surprise, Dr. Vandoren laughed. "Well, I'm glad to have you. Let's get started, shall we?"

I nodded.

"Can you tell me the circumstances surrounding your contraction of HIV, Lucy? It helps me to know your background. And please know that anything you tell me will be kept confidential."

The appointment continued on pretty much like that; it was more of a conversation than an interview, and Dr. Vandoren would respond to certain things I said with questions of her own, occasionally writing things down for her notes. She spent a long time talking with me—I didn't feel like she was in a rush at all.

Then she got to the results of my tests from last week. "You are currently in what we call Stage I of HIV infection, Lucy. If you have to have the virus at all, that's where you want to be. You are asymptomatic, and your CD4 count is just over five hundred. Are you familiar with the term CD4?"

I shook my head.

"You may have heard of T-cells?"

"Yeah, I have." I didn't add that the only thing I really knew about T-cells came from listening to the *Rent* cast album a million times.

"Well, the CD4 is a kind of protein on the surface of the T-cell, which is a white blood cell. In people without HIV or AIDS, the normal CD4 range is usually between six hundred and twelve hundred. The lower the CD4 count, the less capable your immune system is of fighting off infections. When the count drops to below two hundred, that means the patient's condition has progressed to AIDS. We aim to keep the CD4 count above three-fifty in our HIV-positive patients. So the fact that yours is above five hundred is very good news."

My mind was frantically trying to keep track of all of this. It was a lot to try to understand, but I would take this any day over the way Dr. Jackson spoke to me last week. At least Dr. Vandoren was treating me like an individual capable of actual thought.

"We also ran the RNA viral load test. When you have HIV, the virus actually makes copies of itself while inside your body. The lower the virus levels in your system, the better. The higher your viral load, the quicker the HIV progresses. This is why it's important to always have protected intercourse, even if your partner is also HIV positive. You can pass it back and forth to each other, which causes the virus to replicate exponentially."

Whoa, I didn't know that. I'd figured having HIV was kind of like getting pregnant—once you had it, that was it. I didn't know you could keep getting infected over and over again. The thought was…upsetting.

"Your RNA viral load count came in at over one hundred thousand, which is fairly high, but don't get too concerned."

Fairly high? Too late, I was already getting concerned.

"The count is always higher in the initial months after infection, because the HIV is just taking hold in your body and it's reproducing at a rapid rate. Within the next couple of months, it *will* decline and level off." She paused. "Do you understand all of this?"

"I think so," I said.

"Don't hesitate to ask questions if you think of any, okay?"

"Okay."

We moved into an exam room, and she did a physical on me. The entire exam process was a lot more comfortable than last week. Dr. Vandoren told me what she was doing and what she was looking for and asked me about myself. She seemed genuinely interested in knowing who I was as a person, not just a patient. Then she asked the nurse to get my parents, and told me to get dressed and meet back in her office. Five minutes later, I was sitting across from Dr. Vandoren's desk again, my dads at my side.

"So, the next step is to determine treatment," Dr. Vandoren said after introducing herself to my dads and explaining the test results to them. "I would like to see you once a month initially, to monitor the decrease in your RNA viral load. Does that sound reasonable?"

I nodded, although the thought of getting eight vials of blood taken every single month wasn't exactly appealing.

"And after the first few months, if everything is going well, we can reduce our meetings to once every three months."

"That sounds good," I said, and meant it. I liked Dr. Vandoren, and I trusted her. I would do whatever she said.

"The last thing I want to discuss with you today, Lucy, is medication. There is a lot of debate throughout the medical community on the best time to begin drug therapy. Some physicians believe it is best to wait until the CD4 count dips below three-fifty, because the side effects of the drugs can be tricky and they want to give their patients as much time as possible without having to deal with them. I, on the other hand, am of the 'hit hard, hit early' school of thought."

"What does that mean?" Dad asked.

"It means that even though Lucy's CD4 count is high, I think it's beneficial to begin medication immediately. We're only thirty or so years into researching this virus, but studies thus far have shown that the death rate is almost twice as high when medication is deferred. If we start Lucy on a therapeutic regimen now, she could live a very long life," Dr. Vandoren said firmly. "However, I can only recommend what I think is best. The decision ultimately lies with you."

"What kind of side effects are we talking about, exactly?" Papa asked.

"As with any drug, they vary from person to person and are difficult to predict, but the more common side effects include rash, headache, fatigue, drowsiness, dizziness, strange dreams, trouble sleeping, diarrhea, and vomiting. But these usually go away after a few weeks. Other more serious possibilities can include loss of fat in your arms, legs, or face, shortness of breath, pancreatic inflammation, and skin discolorations," Dr. Vandoren stated matter-of-factly, without even consulting a cheat sheet.

Dad sucked in his breath. "That doesn't seem very pleasant."

"Which is why many patients decide to defer treatment. However, think of it this way: as unappealing as these possible side effects may seem, for individuals with HIV and AIDS, the ultimate side effect of no medication is death." Her last word echoed around the room.

Oddly, even though she was throwing around words like "death," I felt safe in her hands. I looked to my dads. "What do you think?"

"I think we should start the meds," Dad said, nodding with conviction. "Seth?"

"I agree," Papa said. "But what do *you* think, Lucy?"

I thought about Roxie—nineteen years and still no sign of AIDS. I nodded. "Hit hard, hit early."

31

There's a Fine, Fine Line

Alone again. Naturally.

Wasn't there a song about that? I should have learned to play it—it was my theme song lately.

I didn't hear a single peep from Ty all weekend.

And even though there was so much other stuff—more important stuff—going on, my brainwaves were consumed by him.

Saturday night, I began my medication. I had to take it on an empty stomach, and Dr. Vandoren made it clear that because it could make me feel sick, it was best to take it before bed rather than in the morning. So, starting now, ostensibly for the rest of my life, I would have to stop eating by eight p.m. in order to take the pill at ten.

As I took that first pill, I wasn't thinking about the side effects or what this meant for my life. All I could think about was Ty. Would he notice if I started feeling sick all the time? If he asked me out to dinner, would he think it was weird when I told him I had to go on the early side? Maybe I should keep the prescription bottle hidden, in case he saw it the next time he was in my room…

The pill slid down my throat, and for an instant, everything remained still.

My dads and I looked at each other. It was like we were waiting for something to happen, like I would immediately look healthier or something. Or sicker. But everything was the same.

Papa spoke first.

"All right, then," he said, clasping his hands together. "Anyone up for a movie?"

"Actually, I'm going to head to bed. Love you guys," I said.

"Love you too, honey," Dad and Papa said in unison.

I checked my phone again one more time before crawling into bed, fully aware that Einstein's definition of insanity was repeating the same action over and over and expecting a different result.

• • •

When Lisa came home from the hospital on Sunday, I stayed closed away in my room all day, staring at my computer and waiting for Ty to log on to instant messenger. He didn't. That night, I finally broke down and called him, but it went straight to voicemail. I didn't leave a message. It was an enormous effort just to bring the phone from my ear and press "end call."

I was utterly worn out. I'd spent so much energy thinking about Ty these past two days that I had gone into overdraft. Or maybe it was an effect of the medication. All I knew was that I was exhausted, emotionally and physically.

I laid my head down on my desk and let the barriers down

against the one thought I'd actively been avoiding. *Could Ty really have just been using me to get ahead in his career?* After all, he hadn't come crawling back until I'd gotten the commercial.

But, I weakly argued with myself, he'd seemed so *genuine* when he told me he missed me. He was exactly the same Ty Friday that he'd been when we were officially together. Was he really that good of an actor? Or (and it killed me to even think this) had our entire year-and-a-half-long relationship been an act?

Was being with the best actress in the school really all that mattered to him? Were Elyse and I some sort of *conquests* for him?

I shook the thought from my mind. Our time together was real. It had to be.

But then Monday afternoon rolled around and brought with it a fresh dose of clarity.

Because of the lingering effects of the snowstorm, we'd had a two-hour delay in the morning, and homeroom was canceled. So it was dress rehearsal time before I saw anyone from the drama club.

I was sitting on the edge of the stage lacing up my costume boots when Ty and Elyse walked in. Together. Holding hands.

I almost fell into the orchestra pit.

"What the hell?" I shouted. Everyone stopped what they were doing and stared.

Ty immediately dropped Elyse's hand and I actually saw him glance at the exit, like I was really going to let him escape. Fueled by a much-needed burst of adrenaline, I leapt off the stage and stormed his way. In the seconds it took to reach him and Elyse, understanding took hold of me. My fears had not been unfounded at all. By the time we were actually face to face, I was more scared than mad.

"Follow me," I said, and led them into an isolated hallway. "What's going on?" I asked quietly once we were alone.

Ty's eyes darted around nervously. "I don't know what you're talking about."

"Yes you do, Ty." I nodded toward Elyse. "Does she know?"

Elyse was looking back and forth between us. "Do I know what?"

I stared at Ty and slowly breathed in and out. "I thought you weren't with her anymore?"

"I…changed my mind," he said.

"Right." I nodded slightly. "Because I said I couldn't get you a part in the commercial."

He wouldn't look at me. Nothing more was said for a long second. I was waiting for him to confess or at least offer an explanation. He was probably waiting for me to go away.

"Okay, seriously, *what* is going on?" Elyse asked.

I looked at Ty. "Do you want to tell her or should I?"

He just kept staring at his shoes.

I let out an exasperated sigh and turned to Elyse. "As much as I don't like you, you deserve to know the truth. Ty came over to my house on Friday and we had sex."

Elyse stiffened and audibly sucked in air.

"He told me you guys weren't together anymore," I defended

myself. But then I realized something. He hadn't said they'd broken up. He'd just said things "weren't working." I had substituted my own meaning for his words. Well, no way I was going to admit that now. "Or something to that effect."

Elyse looked to Ty, her face stricken with disbelief. "Is that true?" she whispered.

Ty shrugged. "I don't know, maybe."

"But we were together all weekend. How…how could you do that?"

Oh god. He was such scum. He went right back to her after me. My eyes were suddenly wide open and, for the first time, I saw him clearly. I couldn't believe I'd fallen for his whole charade.

Amazingly, I actually felt bad for Elyse. Her face was sallow, her lower lip trembling, as she waited for him to say something. She was heartbroken.

"Listen, Elyse," I began, not quite knowing what I was going to say. I worked out my own feelings as I spoke. "You actually got the better end of the deal. At least you can still get out early. Imagine how I feel—he had me wrapped around his little finger for almost *two years*." I shook my head, ashamed, thinking about how much I'd loved him, and the part having my heart broken by him played in my decision to go home with Lee. "And then after everything, he shows up on my doorstep, tells me a few lies, and I immediately fall right back in his trap. Trust me, you don't know how lucky you are that you're finding out the truth now."

I moved to place a comforting hand on Elyse's shoulder, but just then there was a loud crash down the hall. My heart stuttered when I saw who had made the noise. Evan was there, his face pale, hastily collecting the sack of prop swords that he had dropped.

"I…uh, sorry," he muttered.

"Evan…I…" I didn't know what to say. How much had he heard?

But before I could form actual words, he turned and ran back in the direction he'd come.

I stood there frozen for a short moment, putting everything together.

Evan had heard me say I had sex with Ty. He was the only person in the school who knew about my HIV. He was scared to even go near me. And now, for all he knew, I'd given it to Ty.

I turned back to Elyse and Ty. "You guys figure out the rest. I gotta go."

I had to find Evan before he said anything to anyone.

32
The Sword of Damocles

I caught up with him backstage, where he was steadfastly laying out the swords on the prop table.

"Evan?" I said softly.

He flinched at the sound of my voice. "I don't want to talk about it, Lucy," he said, not looking up.

"Just let me explain, please. It's not what you think," I pleaded.

His hands froze. "You didn't have sex with him?"

"That's…not what I meant. I just—"

He looked at me then, his eyes scorching. "Then it is what I think. Like I said, I don't want to talk about it." He brushed past me and walked quickly away.

• • •

I was in a panic. Evan was obviously freaked out by what he thought he knew, and he wouldn't let me get close enough to explain that Ty and I had used protection and that there wasn't anything to worry about. Every time I tried to bring it up backstage during the dress rehearsal, either there wasn't enough privacy or he would pretend to be terribly busy doing some mundane prop or costume thing.

Before I knew it, it was time for our fight.

I did a few stretches to loosen up, adjusted my corset, and entered the scene. But I quickly became more interested in Evan's lines than my own.

I'd never seen him act like this. He was so…intense.

"Romeo," he seethed at Ty like a man out for murder, "the love I bear thee can afford no better term than this: thou art a *villain*."

"Tybalt," Ty responded unsurely, apparently as surprised at Evan's sudden passion as I was, "the reason that I have to love thee doth much excuse the appertaining rage to such a greeting. Villain am I none. Therefore farewell. I see thou knowest me not."

"Boy, this shall not excuse the injuries that thou hast done me," Evan shouted back in his face. "Therefore turn and draw!"

What was going on here? It seemed like Evan was using his lines to act out some sort of real-life resentment against Ty. But that didn't make any sense. It was me he had a problem with, not Ty. In his mind, Ty was the victim, not the villain.

Our fight scene began, and immediately I noticed a change. We should have been rehearsing in costumes all along if that was the cure for Evan's hang-ups. He was no longer hesitant. We fell into sync from the very moment our swords collided. Our eyes locked, and as we jousted and tumbled across the stage, it felt almost like therapy, like we were finally liberating ourselves of all our unaired baggage. Our respective inner turmoils manifested themselves through our characters' rivalry.

The fight was everything it was supposed to be—fluid and freeing, angry and beautiful.

It was strange, considering the violent nature of the moment, but as Evan and I fought, I felt a warmth inside that grew larger and hotter the deeper his eyes blazed into mine. My brain didn't understand, but my body seemed to know that, whatever was happening right now, it was good.

But then I was accosted by a tidal wave of dizziness. Out of nowhere, the world blurred and tilted, and I instantly knew it was from the pills. But I couldn't do anything about it right then. It's an unspoken rule of theater that you don't interrupt a dress rehearsal unless you absolutely have to. Besides, I could handle it. I was stumbling and struggling to remain upright, my focus on Evan lost, but I forced myself to keep up with the fight choreography as best I could. Ty was already speaking his next lines, pleading our characters to stop our battle, so all I had to do was get fake-injured, and I could collapse onto the stage, in character, and wait for the dizzy spell to subside.

The blocking of the moment was simple: I was supposed to face sideways, so that when Evan jabbed the empty space next to me it would look to the audience like I was being stabbed. Easy.

But my balance faltered again. On cue, Evan thrust his sword out at me, but we were out of sync now—and instead of slicing the air, he slashed it across my bare upper arm.

Everyone on stage stopped dead in their tracks. I didn't feel the cut in my arm, but I knew it was there. Adrenaline made sure that I had no sensation of anything except my legs turning to jelly and the crash of my butt against the wooden stage floor. People were shouting, and the floor pulsed as Andre pounded up the stage steps.

At last, the dizziness retreated, and I slowly turned my head and looked at the cut. It was more of a gaping gash, sliding up from just above my elbow to just under my shoulder. Blood was everywhere, streaming down my arm in bright red ribbons.

I turned back to find the world had devolved into chaos. Elyse had fainted, and Ty was tending to her. Max and Courtney were running toward me, and Andre was motionless, midway between me and Elyse, as if he didn't know who to take care of first. But it was Evan that I was zeroed in on. He leapt over Elyse and cut off Max and Courtney.

He threw himself on top of me, knocking me backward, and remained there in a protective stance as he drew the sash from around his waist and tied it tightly around my arm.

"I'll call for an ambulance!" Max yelled.

"No!" Evan shouted back firmly, holding up a palm. "Don't call anyone!"

I stared in terror at Evan's hands. They were covered in my blood.

"Evan," I gasped. "Your hands."

"Shhhh," he whispered, and held up a red-stained finger.

"What are you *talking* about?" Max yelled, having reached us now. "I'm calling 911. She needs stitches!"

"I'll take her to the hospital myself," Evan insisted, picking me up. He brought me closer to Max and Courtney and spoke under his breath, so that only the four of us could hear. "Don't let anyone near that," he said, nodding at the puddle of blood on the floor. "Clean it up yourself. Use bleach, make sure you wear gloves, and throw everything away when you're done. Understand?"

Max and Courtney nodded, speechless.

I cradled my arms around Evan's neck as he carried me toward the exit.

"I'm so sorry, Lucy," he whispered, as we left the bloody scene behind.

33
Think of Me

Thirty-two stitches and a prescription for Tylenol with codeine later, I was discharged from the emergency room.

"I still don't understand how this happened. Don't you use fake weapons on stage?" Dad said when he and I met up with Andre and Evan in the waiting room. Papa was at home, on Lisa duty. He was following through with his promise to never leave her alone for the next three months, and it was already driving her crazy. He'd even hired someone to stay with her during the day and canceled the movie channels just to piss her off.

"Yes, of course we do," Andre said, glaring at me and Evan. "Where did you even *get* those swords?"

"In the basement," I mumbled.

Andre's eyebrows pulled together and he thought for a moment. "Were they in a glass case?"

I nodded.

"Dammit, Lucy, those were for display only. They're antiques from the RenFaire museum. You should have checked with me."

He turned to my dad. "If I had known Lucy and Evan weren't abiding by the rules, I certainly would have put a stop to it."

"We're sorry," I said, trying to make amends so we didn't have to keep talking about this. "Aren't we sorry, Evan?"

Evan just nodded. He was staring at my bandaged arm.

"What did the doctors say? Are you still going to be able to be in the show?" Andre was a worried wreck. I felt for the guy—just when the fight scene was finally working, this had to happen.

"The play really does seem to be cursed, doesn't it?" I said, a dopey grin on my face. The painkillers were making me silly. "Just imagine if we'd done *Macbeth.*"

"Lucy, *please* don't talk about theater curses. What are you trying to do, jinx us?" Andre shuddered. "Now, can you be in the show or not?"

"Yes, Andre, I can still be in the show."

"Oh, thank god," he breathed, and gave me a giant hug, being careful of my injured arm.

"All right, let's go home. I've had enough of hospitals to last me awhile," Dad said, leading us toward the exit.

"Um, actually, I think I'm going to ride home with Evan. If that's okay with him," I added.

"Yeah, no problem," Evan agreed after a brief hesitation. It was no use avoiding me anymore, and we both knew it.

Dad looked from me to Evan and back again. "I suppose that's okay," he said. "But come straight home, all right? We have some things to talk about."

"I will."

He gave me a big squeeze. "See you at home, honey."

• • •

"Are you okay?" Evan asked the moment we were alone.

I nodded. "I'll be fine. Probably gonna have a nasty scar, but otherwise I'm okay."

"I am *so* sorry. I can't believe I did that. I don't know what happened."

"It wasn't your fault, Evan. Honestly. Don't beat yourself up about it."

"Lucy, I was the one holding the sword. I don't know who else's fault it would have been."

I smiled. "Well, you more than made up for it. Thanks for bringing me to the hospital."

"I just thought that if an ambulance came you would have had to tell them about the HIV, and I know you don't want anyone to know," he said quietly, looking down at his lap.

He was right. When I got to the emergency room, one of the first things the nurses asked me was if I had any allergies to medications or major health issues. I nervously told them about my HIV status, and they barely even blinked. But if I'd had to disclose that information to EMTs with all my castmates standing around and watching, I don't know what I would have done. Evan had saved me.

I studied him closely. He seemed like he meant what he said. And he'd put himself in danger in order to protect my secret. To think that just a few hours ago I was worried about him telling people...

"You shouldn't have touched my blood," I whispered, my stomach still tied up in knots about that.

"I know. But I wasn't thinking. I just wanted to help you," he admitted.

"Do you have any cuts on your hands?" *Please say no,* I added silently.

Evan held up his hands for me to see. "Nope. Perfectly intact."

I breathed a sigh of relief. "Good. But maybe…I think you should probably still get tested in a month or so, just in case." It pained me to even think the words, let alone say them. I wouldn't be able to live with myself if something happened to Evan because of me.

"Yeah, okay," Evan said.

We sat there, letting the seriousness of the situation sizzle and pop in the contained atmosphere. Why was it that all of Evan's and my most important conversations took place in a parked car?

"So I think Max and Courtney probably know something's up," he said, finally breaking the silence. "I'm really sorry. I know you didn't want them to know anything. I was just trying to think on my feet and I thought them knowing would be better than Elyse…or Ty."

I shook my head reassuringly. "No, you did the right thing. Thank you." Then his reluctance to say Ty's name registered in my brain. "About what you overheard in the hallway today…"

Evan looked away. "It's none of my business."

"No, it's okay. I know you're freaked out about it. But you should know that I didn't put Ty at risk. I was really careful and we used a cond—"

"Lucy, please. I don't need the details," he cut me off.

"Sorry. I just want you to understand that you don't have to worry about Ty."

"Lucy, I couldn't care less about Ty."

I blinked. "But you were so upset…"

He looked me directly in the eye. "I was upset because you were with someone else, not because of Ty's health."

Wait. What?

I stared at him, my heartbeat picking up speed.

"Is that…why you were shouting in Ty's face during rehearsal?" I said slowly, piecing it all together.

"You caught that?" He looked sheepish.

"I think *everyone* caught that."

"Oh. Well, yeah, I hate that guy."

"But you don't like me anymore!" I cried. "You won't even look at me half the time!"

"Lucy, I'm in love with you," Evan said, embarrassed. "I'm *always* looking at you. I'm just good at hiding it, I guess."

I gaped at him.

He looked down. "I'm so sorry about the way I treated you. I was just…scared." The way he said it, it was like he couldn't believe he was even admitting it.

"But you're…not scared anymore?" I nudged.

He sighed. "I still am. But I've done a lot of reading, and I think I understand it all a little better now." He took my hand.

As I considered our entwined fingers, Evan's thumb stroking the back of my hand, I thought back to the last time I'd tried to touch him, the last time we were in a parked car together. It was only five weeks ago, but it seemed so much longer. So much had happened since then; things were different now. And, judging from the way Evan's warm skin felt against mine, those things weren't all bad.

"But I was a total jerk to you, and I get it if you don't feel the same way about me. Or if you're still into Ty or whatever."

"I'm definitely *not* still into Ty."

Evan's eyes lit up. "Really?"

"Really." But then a searing shot of pain coursed through my injured arm, reminding me that things still weren't exactly simple. I exhaled. "But I don't know, Evan…"

His thumb stopped moving. "You don't know what?"

"I don't know if you and I could ever really work. It's complicated."

"Because of the HIV?"

"Well, yeah. That's the big thing, obviously. I'm in for a lifetime of health problems and medication side effects and doctors' appointments and group meetings. It's a lot to deal with. But also because you really hurt me, and honestly, I'm still working through that. And I know you said you've done a lot of research and all that, but I can't help but worry that you'll always be a little skittish around me."

Evan slowly released my hand, nodding. "Okay. I understand." He started the car and began driving in the direction of my house.

I was a mess inside. I wanted to be with him. I wanted to kiss him and have him hold me and be loved by someone as good as him. But what I said was the truth, and I had to take care of me now.

"But thank you," I said after a while. "For everything you did today. I mean it—I'll never forget it."

He kept his eyes on the road and didn't respond.

Before long we were pulling up my driveway.

"I'll see you tomorrow," I said, getting out of the car. "Thanks for the ride."

"Lucy, wait," he called out, just as I was about to close the door. I swung it open again and bent down to look at him. "Just…think about it, okay?"

I gave a tiny smile. "Okay."

34
Don't Cry for Me, Argentina

Dad and Papa were waiting for me when I went inside the house, identical masks of concern superglued on their faces.

"What happened?" Dad asked.

It took me a second to realize he was talking about the accident at school and not about what had just passed between me and Evan. "You already know what happened—I got sliced up with a sword."

"Come on, Lucy, you know what I mean. Was anyone exposed?"

The image of Evan's hands saturated red flashed before my eyes, and I winced. *It's okay*, I reminded myself. *He didn't have any open cuts. He'll be fine.*

"No," I lied, and immediately felt a spasm of guilt. I hated lying to my dads. But they couldn't know how badly I'd screwed up. Trying to shift the direction of the conversation, I added, "But I did get really dizzy on stage today. That's kind of what caused the accident."

Papa's jaw clenched. "Is that the first side effect you've felt?"

"I don't know. I've been really tired lately, but that could be caused by a number of things." I shrugged. "It wasn't so bad. Or it wouldn't have been if I hadn't been in close proximity to sharp metal objects." I grinned.

"It's not funny, Lucy," Papa said.

"No, I know. But it could be a lot worse," I pointed out. A little dizziness and fatigue seemed like the least offensive of any of the side effects Dr. Vandoren had listed. I'd take them over chronic bouts of diarrhea any day.

"How's your arm?" Dad asked.

I shrugged again. "'Tis not so deep as a well," I quoted Mercutio, and headed toward the stairs.

"By the way, Max called," Dad said.

I dug my heels into the carpet and spun around. "He did? What did he say?"

"He wanted to see if you were okay. He sounded worried."

Worried. About me? Or was he freaked out about the whole don't-let-anyone-touch-Lucy's-blood thing?

Probably best not to call him back tonight. I needed time to figure out what the hell I was going to say.

• • •

I still hadn't managed to come up with a believable explanation when I found Courtney and Max waiting at my locker the next morning. I almost escaped back the way I came, but I saw them see me.

I swallowed nervously and cautiously approached. "Haven't seen you guys around these parts in a while," I said.

They both just stared at me with big, fretful eyes. Yeah, they definitely knew something was up.

"How's your arm?" Max asked.

I patted the thick bandage under my sweater. "I'll live."

"I called you last night," he said.

"I know."

"Oh. Okay." Max's glance darted to Courtney. He gave her a *say something* look.

She cleared her throat. "We, uh, cleaned up the mess yesterday like Evan told us to."

I gave her a tight smile. "Thanks." But I wasn't about to elaborate.

I watched and waited as my two former best friends worked up the courage to ask me the question we all knew was coming.

Turned out Max was the braver one. "So…what was that all about, anyway?" he asked nonchalantly, tracing the floor tile edges with his toe.

Just make something up. Anything, the voice in my head urged.

But my mind was blank. All I was aware of was the endless mob of students flowing up and down the hall, pushing past us, all potential eavesdroppers.

I couldn't tell them the truth, and I couldn't make up a lie. I had no choice—there was only one way to get Max and Courtney off my back. Fighting against every instinct I had, I built up as much courage as I could and let it explode out of me.

"What do you care?" I yelled. "We're not friends anymore, remember?"

Max flinched. "We're just worried about you."

"Oh, all of a sudden you're *worried*. Well, maybe it's too late, Max. Ever think of that?"

He held my gaze. "This isn't you, Lucy."

I let out a short laugh. "How would you know? You have no idea who I am anymore!" I slammed my locker door and left them there, bewildered.

Just keep walking, I ordered myself. *And don't look back.*

The pain stabbing my heart was a thousand times sharper than any sword. But I'd bought myself some time. I would just have to come up with a good lie before they cornered me again.

• • •

The thing was, I hadn't planned on it happening so soon.

I was setting my props backstage when Max tapped me on the shoulder. "Lucy."

I steeled myself for another fight and whirled around to find him and Courtney standing uncomfortably close. I gave them both the evil eye. "What?"

"I talked to Evan," he said with emphasis.

I sucked in my breath sharply, my heartbeat instantly doing the hundred-meter dash.

What did Evan tell him? Did they *know*? What were they thinking right now?

I searched Max's face for clues but came up empty. He was always the best liar out of the three of us, because of his uncanny ability to remain reactionless during pretty much any situation. Courtney's expression, on the other hand, was more revealing. She was chewing on the inside of her cheek—a telltale sign that she was troubled. Yes, something had definitely changed since this morning.

How much had Evan told them? Surely not *everything*. Not after all he went through yesterday just to protect my secret.

I had to find out what they knew.

"We can't talk here," I said. "Come with me."

I coaxed the lighting team out of the light booth and shuffled Max and Courtney inside. We were alone. No chance of anyone overhearing. But that meant there was also nowhere to escape to. I'd never been claustrophobic, but I was suddenly feeling trapped.

I took a few long, deep breaths to steady myself, and then got straight to it. I needed to get out of there as soon as possible. "What did Evan tell you?"

"He didn't say much. Just that it's some sort of…medical issue. And that we should ask you to explain the rest," Max said.

I let out a sigh of relief. A nondescript medical issue. That could mean anything. I could have something totally benign, like hay fever. Or high cholesterol. Or low blood sugar. Yes, that was it! My blood sugar was too low and that was why I'd gotten lightheaded. Evan had just overreacted, he was so sweet—but no. Of course they wouldn't buy that. It didn't even make sense.

"I've been going through it all over and over in my mind," Max continued, scratching his head. "You have some sort of medical issue that is too big for Evan to tell us about. And yesterday he acted like your blood was *dangerous*. The only thing I can think of that makes blood dangerous is AIDS. And I know you don't have that. So what is it, Lucy?"

I felt like I'd been kicked in the gut. He was so close to the truth, and yet he thought it impossible. How could I possibly confirm a truth so unbearable that he refused to even hypothetically consider it?

I met his gaze, my eyes stinging with tears.

Whatever he saw in my face, it made his own expression solemn. I could see him retracing his words, trying to figure out what he'd said that would have made me cry.

Courtney caught on before Max did. "You don't…actually *have* AIDS?"

I looked down and rubbed my eyes hard with the heels of my palms, pushing back the moisture, not caring that I was probably smearing mascara all over my face. When I couldn't stand the stupefied silence any longer, I swallowed the lump in my throat and turned to Courtney. "Not yet," I said. "But I will." If the meds didn't do their job, anyway.

"HIV?" she whispered so softly that it was barely audible.

I nodded, gulping back the tears that were threatening reappearance. Max sank down to the floor in shock and Courtney just stared at me. I quickly looked away—I didn't want to see the moment when disgust replaced the disbelief written on their faces.

"How?" I heard Courtney say.

There was no reason not to tell them the rest now. I fixed my gaze on the lighting board, fiddling with the little dials and knobs as I forced the word to pass through my lips. "Lee."

The gasps of understanding came right away. Even after nearly two months of not speaking, all I had to do was utter one little name, and they understood exactly what I meant.

Just then Andre's voice came through the speaker system announcing five minutes to places, and the lighting crew started pounding on the door. I wasn't even in stage makeup or costume yet—it was the perfect excuse to get the hell out of there. I swiftly unlocked the door and let the displaced techies inside. "We have to go," I muttered, not meeting Max or Courtney's eyes, and bolted toward the balcony exit.

"What the hell did you do to my lighting board?!" one of the board operators yelled. I ignored him and kept running.

But Courtney and Max's footsteps pursued me. "Lucy, wait!" Courtney called out.

I pretended not to hear.

"Lucy! Stop!" she yelled again.

There was something in her voice—something surprisingly authoritative—that made me stop in my tracks.

Here it comes. I held my breath as I braced myself for their hastily devised excuse as to why we couldn't be friends after all.

But without a sound, they wrapped their arms around me and held me tight. All at once, the walls I'd put up around me collapsed and for several long minutes I was enveloped in warmth, security. It was the best feeling in the entire world.

I could have stayed there all day, but we pulled apart at the sound of, "Places!"

That's when I saw the tears in their eyes. "Don't cry," I said. "Please."

Max nodded and cleared his throat. "Come on, Luce," he said, taking my hand, "let's go put on the best show of our lives."

The relief that flooded through me was so great that my radar barely even registered Elyse standing in the shadows of the balcony, her face stricken with pure terror.

35

Happiness

There was no time to stop and catch my breath. After my miraculous reconciliation with Max and Courtney, aka the two most supportive, awesome friends ever, I rushed to get into costume and at least give my makeup a cursory touchup before my big entrance in act 1, scene 4.

Between costume changes and scenery changes and everyone running around backstage working to keep up the pace, I couldn't think about anything but the play. But that was good. I was glad to have something as permanent and timeless as Shakespeare to keep me grounded.

Evan caught up with me at intermission. "Max cornered me," he confessed guiltily. "He demanded to know what's going on. I didn't know what to say—"

"Evan," I said. "It's okay. I told them."

"You did?"

"Yeah."

"And?"

"And it's all fine."

His face lit up. "See? I *knew* they'd be cool. And you were so worried. You don't give people enough credit, Lucy."

I gave him a look. "That might be true, but I still don't want anyone else finding out."

"Understood," he said with a nod. "So have you given any more thought to what we talked about?"

Honestly, I hadn't. I'd spent the entire night trying to come up with a way to dodge Max and Courtney. But it had only been a day since our conversation, and nothing had changed. "I meant what I said last night, Evan," I said gently. "I need time."

He nodded, a little dejectedly. "Okay. I'll stop asking."

I gave a tiny smile and patted him on the shoulder. "Patience, young grasshopper."

Evan threw up his hands, laughing. "And she quotes *Kung Fu*! I really am in love with this girl."

• • •

Evan and I were forced to replace our fancy swords with prop swords, but we couldn't really object to that. We'd learned our lesson. The prop swords were lighter and easier to use, anyway. And now that we'd resolved our fight scene issues, the show was coming off without a hitch.

Or that was almost true.

No one knew what the hell was up with Elyse. Miss I'm-the-best-actress-in-the-world suddenly seemed to be battling a severe case of premature stage fright. She kept having to call out for lines—lines that she had known perfectly yesterday—and she missed her cue not once but *four* times.

I watched in delight from the wings as she fell flat on her face time and time again. Finally, someone other than me was messing everything up. It was just icing on the cake that it happened to be Elyse.

Andre decided at the last minute to turn the rehearsal into a double. He still refused to accept that the show was cursed and was on a fool's quest to do whatever it took to get the production on its feet.

At six p.m., I called home.

"Dad?" I said. "I can't go to the meeting tonight. Andre called a double rehearsal."

"Forget it, Lucy. You haven't been to a meeting in a week. Tell Andre you have a prior obligation."

"You don't understand—the show opens in three days! I have to be here."

"Sorry, honey. No dice," he said.

"But what am I going to tell Andre?" I protested.

"Tell him he doesn't know how lucky he is that your parents are even still letting you be in the play after *his* negligence landed you in the hospital and with thirty stitches in your arm," Dad retorted.

"Thirty-two," I mumbled.

"Exactly."

"There's no way I'm telling him that."

"I really don't care what you tell him, Lucy. But you're not missing the meeting."

I sighed. "Fine. See you at home."

I fed Andre some line about having a follow-up doctor's appointment for my arm, and he let me go without protest. Dad must have been right about him feeling responsible for my injury, because when Chris Mendoza asked permission to go home early because he had to babysit his little sister, Andre told him to get back on stage and stop bothering him with his petty requests.

Thirty minutes later, I was in the car with my dads and Lisa, Manhattan-bound.

I hated having to share the backseat with Lisa. Every now and then I'd catch the reflection of her bratty pout in the window, and I had to stifle the urge to give her a swift roundhouse kick to the mouth.

"Is *anyone* going to explain to me where we're going?" she whined.

"All you need to know is that Lucy has somewhere to be at eight, and we're escorting her," Papa replied serenely.

"But why do *I* have to come?"

Papa gave her a pitying look in the rearview mirror. "I'm just going to go ahead and let you figure that one out on your own, Lisa. Now, I know *thinking* is not your strong suit, but look on the bright side—at least you'll have this little puzzler to keep you occupied for the next hour or so."

I smiled. I was really enjoying this new take-no-crap attitude of his.

* * *

I was glad when we got to the meeting a little early, because I wanted to talk to Roxie. I found her arranging store-brand cookies on a platter, her emerald green fingernails twinkling under the church basement's lights.

"Hey," I said.

She looked up in surprise. "Lucy! You're back!"

"Yeah, sorry. The snowstorm made traveling difficult."

"Oh, that's right. I always forget you come here from upstate."

"Westchester is hardly *upstate*," I said. "It's only twenty-five miles away."

Roxie laughed. "Sorry, didn't mean to offend. But for real, I thought you were seriously pissed at me."

I grimaced, remembering the last meeting. "I was. Actually, I still kind of am. Why did you do that, again?"

"I guess I thought it would help. My bad." She looked up at me sheepishly.

"If I'm being honest…it might have." I explained all about my fight with Lisa, and how we found out Lisa had been doing drugs this whole time.

"Whoa," Roxie said, wide-eyed. "You've had a busy week."

"Oh, that's not even the half of it," I said, and rolled up my sleeve to show her my battle wound. I told her about starting the meds, and what had happened with Evan and then with Max and Courtney. But I kept the Ty stuff to myself. I knew I shouldn't have slept with him, for many reasons, and I was trying to convince myself that entire snowy Friday afternoon had never happened.

I didn't know it then, but moving on from that mistake was going to be harder than I could have imagined.

I got home that night to a message waiting on the house line voicemail.

"Hello, this is Mr. Fisher, from Eleanor Senior High," the voice said.

My principal? Why would he be calling?

"I'd like for Miss Moore to come meet with me in my office tomorrow morning before school. Say, seven a.m.? Thank you, see you then." The message ended.

My dads and I stared at each other. What could *that* be all about?

36

(Ya Got) Trouble

I smoothed the wrinkles from the front of my skirt, took a deep breath, and knocked on Mr. Fisher's office door. I'd talked my dads into staying home, but now I was regretting that decision. I had no idea what faced me on the other side of that door and I was suddenly feeling the need for backup.

I hadn't even thought that Mr. Fisher knew who I was. I was a straight-A, problem-free honors student who never cut class and hung out with the drama kids. Maybe this was something he did with all the juniors, as a pre-SAT, pre-college application catch-up session? No, if he had the entire 600-member class to get through, the meeting would surely be during school hours and scheduled far in advance. This was an emergency.

The door swung open and Mr. Fisher looked down at me. I'd never been this close to him before—he was a lot taller than I'd thought, well over six feet. His mustache was redder than the rest of his hair, and his glasses were smudged.

"Please come in, Miss Moore. Thank you for taking the time to meet with me," he said, and closed the door behind us.

I wasn't aware I'd had a choice. "Sure," I said.

"Have a seat," he said, and gestured to the high-backed leather chair across from his desk, before sitting in his own high-tech office chair. I hoisted myself into my seat, my feet dangling several inches above the floor. I wondered if he purposely kept this chair here to make the students sitting in it feel small. "You're probably wondering what this is all about."

"Actually, yeah," I admitted. "Did I do something wrong?"

He hesitated, and I realized for the first time that *he* was nervous too. "No, no, no one is in trouble here," he said.

"Okay…"

"I've received some rather…sensitive information, and I would like to speak with you about it," he said, still avoiding specifics.

My eyes narrowed. "Regarding?"

"Regarding your…health." He swallowed and forced himself to look me in the eye. "I assume you know what I mean?"

Of course I knew what he meant. But what I didn't know was how the hell the *principal of my school* found out. My face flamed with alternating flashes of embarrassment and betrayal.

"Who told you?" I whispered.

"I'm afraid I'm not at liberty to say," he said awkwardly.

I blinked. "Why?"

"There are certain confidentiality laws that come into play here…"

I stared at him for a long moment in shock, trying to figure out what to do. "Mr. Fisher," I said slowly, "if you're not going to tell me anything, why did you call me here?"

He cleared his throat. "I wanted to run something by you. As far as I know, you're the first student at this school with… you know."

"HIV," I said pointedly. If he was allowed to make me feel uncomfortable, I was going to do the same to him.

"Indeed. Well, I thought this could be an excellent teaching opportunity. What would you think about leading an assembly on the importance of personal responsibility? I think you're the perfect example of how something like this could happen to anyone. We could get the health teachers involved if you'd like, but I think the kids would really respond to you."

I couldn't believe this. I shouldn't have to deal with this kind of crap, especially in my own school.

The sound of foot traffic outside the office door gradually increased as busloads of students entered the building. Students who, if Mr. Fisher got his way, would soon be privy to my secret.

I kept my response simple. "No."

The corners of his mouth turned down just a bit. "May I ask why not?" Mr. Fisher said.

"I don't think I would feel very comfortable being put on the spot like that," I said.

Mr. Fisher was nodding, not looking particularly dissuaded by my refusal. "What if I told you," he said with a knowing air, "that if you reconsidered, you would be excused from Phys. Ed. for the remainder of your tenure at this school?"

"No gym?"

Mr. Fisher chuckled. "It's my understanding that most girls your age don't particularly enjoy the Phys. Ed. requirement."

"But don't I need the credits in order to graduate?"

"Participating in the assembly would make you eligible for an independent study health credit," he explained.

For one eternal, beautiful second, I considered never having to be subjected to the hell-on-earth known as dodgeball ever again. I had to admit, I was tempted to accept the offer. But there was something about Mr. Fisher's self-satisfied smile that wasn't quite right, and I began to feel uneasy. Something else was going on here…

And then I saw it.

Mr. Fisher wasn't trying to be nice. He was just trying to cover his own ass. He probably thought he'd concocted the perfect plan: get the girl with HIV to out herself in front of the whole school under the guise of "education," and then deliberately keep her out of gym class so the other students wouldn't be at risk. He'd be seen by thousands of parents as a man of action, the one who saved their children from certain death. The PTA would probably crown him Principal of the Year.

Here it is, I realized with a start. My first run-in with real-world, hard-and-fast discrimination. I'd thought I'd been prepared for this moment, that when something like this actually happened to me,

I'd know what to do. How naïve I'd been. Roxie's warnings, the stories shared at the meetings, and the shapeless, colorless hypothetical were nothing compared with the cutting reality.

I felt contaminated, worthless.

Somehow, I managed to keep my gaze level and my voice calm. I had something to say, and I needed to make sure he heard every word. "Mr. Fisher, thank you for the...tempting offer, but my answer is still no. I don't want to be treated differently from the other students. This is a public school, and I have the right to not be singled out or discriminated against for any reason. I'll just have to suffer through gym class like every other student."

I paused, carefully considering my next words. I'd never spoken to an authority figure like this. He was my principal, after all. But still, he had to understand how wrong he was.

"If you ever call me in for another meeting like this, or give me special treatment in any way because of what you know, I will sue you. My father is a lawyer, Mr. Fisher, a really good one."

He nodded, his skin gone white.

"And another thing—I'm a good student, and I've done my homework. Since you clearly take confidentiality laws seriously, here's one for you: according to New York State law, you are forbidden from disclosing my HIV-positive status to anyone. Not the school nurse, not your wife, not anybody. My health is no one's business but my own." Just a little nugget I'd picked up from reading Roxie's informational pamphlets. "Do you understand?"

"Of course, of course," he said, unnerved at having lost control of the conversation.

"Good." Then a terrible thought occurred to me. "You haven't told someone already, have you?"

"No," he assured me. "I wanted to speak with you first."

I gave him a penetrating stare, letting him know I saw right through him. He meant he wanted to make sure I'd go along with his little plan first.

"I'm sorry, I've clearly upset you," Mr. Fisher said quickly, waving his hands as if to wipe away the entire conversation. "I assure you that was not my intention—"

I stood to leave just as the first bell sounded.

"I have to get to class," I said, and booked it out of there, the nervous layer of sweat on my forehead catching the breeze of the hallway.

• • •

I made a beeline to homeroom, not even bothering to drop my coat off at my locker first. I grabbed Evan, Max, and Courtney by the sleeves and yanked them, stunned, into the hall. My head was still spinning after my meeting with the principal.

"Are you okay?" Courtney said.

"No, I'm not *okay*," I snapped. "Who did you tell?"

The three of them just stared back at me.

"One of you said something to someone, and I need to know who."

Still no one said anything. Fine, I would grill them individually then.

I turned to my right. "Evan?"

He looked back at me, offended. "Jeez, Lucy, I thought I would have earned your trust by now."

"That's not an answer," I pointed out.

He rolled his eyes. "Of course I didn't tell anyone."

I stared him down for a few more seconds, and then, satisfied with what I saw, moved on. "Max? Who did you tell?"

"No one, I swear!" he said.

"No one?"

"No one."

"Swear on your Daniel Radcliffe–autographed *Equus* Playbill," I commanded.

"Come on, Luce, are you serious with this?"

"Just do it."

"Fine." Max raised his right hand. "I swear on my Daniel Radcliffe–autographed *Equus* Playbill that I did not tell anyone. Jeez."

That left Courtney. I turned to my left. "Who did you tell, Court?"

"Lucy, you know me. I would never tell anybody *anything* that you told me in confidence. You know that," she said, her voice trembling slightly.

I heaved a frustrated sigh. "Well *somebody* told *somebody*, and I know it wasn't my dads. You three are the only other people in Eleanor Falls who know."

MY LIFE AFTER NOW

"Can you please just tell us what's going on?" Max asked.

I lowered my voice. "Mr. Fisher just asked me to do a freaking safe-sex assembly for the entire school."

"*What?*" Evan said. "Who told him?"

I gave him an annoyed look. "That's what I'm trying to figure out."

• • •

I spent the entire day wracking my brain. Max, Courtney, and Evan swore up and down that they hadn't said a word, and I believed them. So who could have told? It didn't make any sense—no one else even knew.

I called Roxie during lunch.

"I know this is going to sound paranoid," I said, "but you don't know anyone in Eleanor Falls, do you?"

"What's Eleanor Falls?" she said.

"It's the town where I live."

"Nope. Never heard of it. Why, what's up?"

"Somebody told the principal of my school about me being positive. And I can't for the life of me figure out who the hell it would have been."

Roxie's voice suddenly got serious. "Lucy, that's not good. You need to find out who did it, and soon. If they told your principal, they'll tell the whole school. And you do *not* want that."

"I know, I know. I'm working on it." I sighed. "I'll see you Thursday." I hung up the phone and rubbed my temples in frustration.

No one knew. And if no one knew, no one could have told

Mr. Fisher. But Mr. Fisher had obviously been told. So what was I missing?

Obviously someone had found out somehow. I didn't know how, but that wasn't the point anymore. I had to stop focusing solely on the limited pool of people who I thought knew and start thinking about who would actually *do* a thing like that. I mean, really, going and tattling to the principal? That was low.

And then, suddenly, halfway through Honors English, it hit me. Of course. There was only one person who hated me that much.

37

Sit Down, You're Rockin' the Boat

Elyse St. James.

It all made so much sense.

She'd been there on the balcony yesterday after I'd run out of the light booth, and I'd stupidly paid her no attention. But now that I thought about it, she'd looked utterly freaked.

And then she'd been so spacy all throughout rehearsal. Maybe this was why. She must have somehow overheard my conversation with Max and Courtney and then went running to the principal.

She had crossed a major line, and she was *not* going to get away with it.

I stormed into the women's dressing room. "Ladies, could you leave me and Elyse alone for a minute, please?" I announced through gritted teeth.

The girls began to protest, but when they caught a glimpse of my face, they quickly backed out of the room. I didn't dare tear my eyes away from Elyse's petrified expression in order to glance in the mirror, but I wouldn't have been surprised if there was actual smoke steaming from my ears. I was *furious*.

I locked the dressing room door and blocked it with my body, so there was no chance for her to escape.

"Why did you do it?" I demanded, my hands balled up into fists and hanging heavily at my sides.

"I…I d-don't know what you're t-talking about," she stammered. Her stage makeup was thick, and there was a line of black eyeliner on only one of her eyes. She looked like an unfinished puppet.

"Oh, cut the crap, Elyse. We both know that you know exactly what I'm talking about. Why would you *do* that?"

She avoided my gaze. "I don't know," she mumbled.

There it was! An admission of guilt.

"Oh, I'm pretty sure you do know," I countered. "Going to the administration about another student's private business isn't something you just do for kicks. So please, enlighten me."

No response.

"Elyse!"

She didn't even look up. I obviously wasn't getting through to her. I raked my hands through the roots of my hair, forced myself to lower my voice a notch, and tried a different tactic. "Look, I think we owe it to each other to at least be honest with one another." Total BS, of course, but if it worked…

Silence.

ARRGGH!!

"Okay, how about this," I said, grasping at straws. "Whatever is said in this room over the next few minutes goes in the vault and will never be spoken of again by either of us."

Still nothing.

I couldn't handle this. I felt like I was trying to elicit emotion from a brick wall. I knew it was pointless to keep trying, but I simply could not leave this room without answers. I needed to know why she was so intent on ruining my life. I would *never* do what she did, not even to my worst enemy.

"Please," I begged, mortified when my voice cracked. "Please, Elyse. Just help me understand." I was so tired of all of this garbage. This moment, right here and now, was the perfect metaphorical representation of everything I'd been through this school year: me, locked in a tiny room, going slowly insane as I fruitlessly fought and screamed and begged and pleaded for an explanation, for some small lump of truth that would shed some light on *why*. I slid down the door to the floor and rested my cheek on my knees.

The second hand on the wall clock ticked rhythmically.

At long last, Elyse spoke. "I did it because I'm scared."

I lifted my head up. "Scared about what?"

"Ty had sex with you, and then he had sex with me," she said simply, leaving me to deduce the rest.

I rubbed my eyes and the little gold spots appeared and then scattered, making my vision, and the meaning behind Elyse's words, clearer. "So you're worried about—"

"Do I have it now too?" she finished, her voice shaking.

Was *that* what this was all about? "No, of course you don't have it. Ty and I used protection."

"But what if the condom didn't work?"

"It did."

"But what if it didn't?" she said again indignantly.

"It didn't break if that's what you're asking."

"But what if it didn't work for another reason?"

I was beginning to get annoyed, but I tried not to let it show. "Condoms do work. That's why everyone always says to have 'safe sex.' If they didn't work, they wouldn't be considered safe, would they?"

She thought about that for a moment. "Well, what about kissing?"

"What about it?"

"What if you gave it to him that way?"

I pressed my lips together, befuddled. "You do know you can't spread it by kissing, right?"

"I mean, yes, I've heard that, but how am I supposed to know what to believe?" she said.

"Elyse," I said calmly. "Trust me. You have nothing to worry about. I swear."

She looked me directly in the eyes for the first time then. "Are you sure?"

"Yes, I'm sure." I paused as she exhaled in relief. "So that's why you told Mr. Fisher? Because you were scared you got it?"

"Yeah."

"That doesn't make sense."

"But it was the only thing I could think to do. I wanted revenge."

That still didn't make any sense. "What did you think he was going to do? Give me detention?"

She shrugged weakly. "I thought maybe he would tell the school board and they'd kick you out of school or something."

"But…Elyse, if you thought you had it too, then wouldn't they have done the same thing to you?"

"Well, I never said it was a thought-out plan."

I almost laughed, but the gravity of the moment pressed down on me again. "Did you tell anyone else?" I asked.

Elyse shook her head. "Ty and I aren't speaking, and my parents would kill me if they found out I was having sex," she admitted.

"What about your friends?"

Her shoulders slumped down a little. "I haven't really gotten to know many people here. Everyone's already in their little cliques and no one ever seems to want to talk to me."

I took a second to reinforce my resolve. There was no way I was going to let her make me feel bad for her. "You know, you don't really make it easy for people to like you. You're pretty…intense. Since we're being honest."

She just shrugged. "I don't know how else to be."

Wait a second—how had this conversation drifted to *her* problems? "How did you find out about me, anyway?" I asked, resolute to get this discussion back on track.

"I knew something weird was going on because you and Courtney and Max were being all secretive. When I saw you go into the light booth, I followed you up there. I was curious."

There's a difference between being curious and being nosy, I thought. But I kept my mouth shut.

She continued. "I sweet-talked one of the techies into lending me his headset. The microphone was on in the booth, so I could hear everything you said."

I mentally slapped myself in the forehead. How could I have been so stupid?

We fell back into silence then, both lost in our own thoughts.

I took my time looking around the cluttered dressing room, at the bizarre and eclectic collection of costumes and props and show posters from years past. An old Macbeth head, impaled on a stick and outfitted with an Annie wig, hung from the ceiling. I shook my head. My life was too weird.

Finally I nodded toward the clock. The dress rehearsal was due to start in a few minutes, and the entire female half of the cast had been banished from the dressing room. "I guess we should get going."

Elyse nodded and stood up. "Right. The show must go on."

"Don't forget to do your other eye," I reminded her.

She looked in the mirror. "Oh yeah. Thanks."

I watched as she resumed her makeup application. Part of me was actually glad that we'd had this conversation, if only to prove that Elyse was human after all. A downright irritating human maybe, but also a marginally less vile, somewhat more relatable one. "Elyse?"

"Yeah?"

"Please don't tell anyone what you know. Especially Ty." If he learned the truth, he would be furious—and rightfully so. He didn't have any reason to keep my secret after what I'd done. It wouldn't be long before the entire drama club knew, and soon after that, the whole school.

Elyse turned from the mirror and gave me a closed-lipped smile. "I guess you're just going to have to trust me," she said.

I took a deep breath and nodded. What other choice did I have?

38
Let Me Entertain You

"Fifteen to places!" the stage manager announced to the women's dressing room.

"Thank you, fifteen!" we responded in chorus.

I applied another layer of fire-engine red lipstick and stepped back to survey myself in the full-length mirror. Calf-high lace-up boots? Check. Red corset and prop sword? Check. Exposed upper arm threaded with dozens of black stitches? Check.

I grinned. I was going to be the most badass Mercutio this play had ever seen.

The energy backstage was electric, the way it can only be on opening night. I ran my hands along the thick, royal blue curtain until I found a breach and peeked, sleuth-like, out into the house. It was a sold-out show, and most seats were already occupied, but I sifted through the dense crowd until I found my people. Dad and Papa, having bought their tickets months ago, were sitting fourth row center, an enormous bouquet of roses laid across both of their laps. Lisa was a few rows behind them on the far side aisle. Papa kept glancing back every few seconds to make sure she was still there.

My attention shifted up to the balcony, where I located Roxie, her little brother Alex, June, Ahmed, and at least six or seven other members of the support group. Roxie had canceled tonight's meeting so they could all come support me. My stomach turned over with a swell of appreciation as I watched them eagerly reading their programs and chatting.

"Cheater," said a voice from behind, making me jump.

I quickly pulled the curtain closed and turned to find Evan standing there, a smirk on his face. Something stirred in me as my eyes drank him in. His white shirt was unlaced at the neck, his hair molded into deliberate disarray, his sword slung coolly over his shoulder. But I quickly told myself to snap out of it. So he looked good in his costume. It didn't mean I should jump right back into a relationship with the guy.

"What?"

"You're not supposed to sneak a look at the audience before the curtain goes up," he said. "Takes all the fun out of it."

"Speak for yourself," I said, grinning. "I think knowing how many people are out there makes it *more* exciting."

He rolled his eyes.

"So, break a leg tonight," I said.

"You too. Or should I say 'pop a stitch'?"

"Don't even think it!" I said, instinctively checking to make sure my stitches were secure. "More bloodshed on this stage is the last thing we need."

"You'll get no argument from me there," he agreed.

Max and Courtney joined us then. They looked so cute, in their matching powder blue Capulet and Lady Capulet costumes.

"Damn, Luce, you look hot," Max said, eyeing me with raised eyebrows. Then he got a little mischievous glint in his eye and conspicuously turned to Evan. "Doesn't she look hot, Evan?"

"*Max!*" I hissed, before Evan could say anything. I shot Max an I'm-going-to-kill-you look. "Cut it out," I mouthed.

Max just batted his eyelashes and looked back at me innocently.

"You really do look good, though, Lucy," Courtney said. "Way better than this *contraption* I'm strapped into."

I giggled. Her dress was pretty huge. But it looked good on her, in a stately sort of way. Perfect for the character. "Steven Kimani won't be able to take his eyes off of you," I assured her with a grin.

At the mere mention of Steven's name, Courtney's eyes got all dreamy and she was beaming like a love-struck schoolgirl. Which, I guess, was what she was. "He sent me flowers back-stage," she said.

"Good!" I said with approval. "He'd better keep it up too, or he'll have the wrath of me to contend with." I patted my sword meaningfully.

"Ooh, scary!" Max said mockingly.

"Places!" the stage manager yelled, crossing the stage with an authoritative stride while simultaneously adjusting the frequency on her headset. "Places, everyone! Right now!"

The four of us took a second for a pre-show group hug and then dispersed to our respective places in the wings. I didn't have to be on stage for a few scenes yet, so I stood off to the side and closed my eyes, letting my head fill up with the beautiful sounds of flats being wheeled out and the flurry of heels clacking against the wooden floor and scores of excited whispers and the stage manager murmuring cues to the light booth and orchestra pit.

"Break a leg, baby," a disembodied male voice interrupted the peaceful drone of stage noises. I squinted through the darkness and was just able to make out the outlines of Ty and Elyse a few feet in front of me. They must not have noticed me standing here.

"You too," she responded, tapping him playfully on the nose. "I love you."

"Love you more," Ty crooned.

"No, I love *you* more!" Elyse countered.

"I love you the *most*!" he said right back, and Elyse giggled.

Hmph, I thought. *Guess they made up.* But the observation was wonderfully free of any bitterness or animosity. Those two could have each other for all I cared.

It did fleetingly occur to me that, now that they were back together, Elyse might tell Ty about my being positive. But I couldn't worry about that now because all at once the orchestra began playing and the curtain was raised to the sound of applause.

A profound thrill coursed through me and I shivered with excitement. There was truly nothing else like this in the world.

Stephanie Gilmore, who was playing the Chorus, stepped into the spotlight and spoke the prologue directly to the audience. "Two households, both alike in dignity, in fair Verona, where we lay our scene. From ancient grudge break to new mutiny, where civil blood makes civil hands unclean."

A grin spread across my face. We were underway.

• • •

It was magic. That was the only explanation.

The play that I'd been so certain was cursed, the play that had *never once* run smoothly in rehearsal, turned out to be perfect in every possible way. By some divine interference, the cast and crew had come together to create something so much bigger than a high school drama production. This was art.

Even *I* was convinced that Elyse and Ty were meant to be together.

• • •

When the time came for our fight, I gave Evan a quick wink with my upstage eye. We so had this. We fell into step and waged battle on each other. The lights boring down on us had me sweating through my makeup, and I was crying out with each slash of the sword like a tennis player serving a ball. Again and again our weapons collided with ferocity, inducing involuntary gasps and shrieks of anxiety from the audience. I'd never had so much fun in my life.

But then I suffered my mortal wound and everything changed.

Though I'd said these very lines countless times before, suddenly every word I said seemed to be infused with double-meaning.

Ask for me tomorrow and you shall find me a grave woman.
I am peppered, I warrant, for this world.
A plague o' both your houses!

I fell to the floor as real tears fled down my face.

They have made worms' meat of me.
I have it, and soundly, too.
Your houses!

Epiphany burst behind my eyelids like fireworks, and everything was abruptly, staggeringly in focus. I lay there, still as a portrait, as the other players continued on without me. But my mind was anything but quiet.

A plague. There was no better word for it. Call it a virus or a disease or an infection. Call it whatever you wanted, but this was truly what it was. A plague. A cureless, indiscriminating, unflinching plague.

I had it. And soundly too.

• • •

The curtain came down, the crowd still on their feet and going wild, and the entire drama club exploded into self-congratulatory celebration. When Andre finally made it past the adoring public and backstage, we quieted down so he could make his traditional post-performance speech.

"I have only one note tonight," he said, deadpan. "Don't. Change. *Anything!*"

We erupted in cheers again, and the party resumed. But I waited for an opening, and when I saw it, snuck away. There was something I had to do.

I quickly changed out of my costume and emerged from the dressing room with my stage makeup still on, hoping I hadn't missed him. But I was brought up short when I found Evan leaning against the wall, waiting for me.

"Oh. Hi," I said. I glanced around, but it was just the two of us. Everybody else was still on the stage. "Why aren't you back there whooping it up with everyone?"

"I saw you duck out. Wanted to see if you were okay," he said.

I blinked. "Why? Do I seem not okay?"

He considered the question. "You seem fine," he admitted. "But you're pretty good at hiding how you're really feeling, so that doesn't really mean anything. It seemed like something…*happened* to you during the show."

How could he possibly have picked up on that? I'd stayed in character the whole time, I was sure of it.

I searched Evan's face and what I saw did funny things to my heartbeat. Earnestness. Compassion. Understanding. Love.

He really did care about me.

"Trust you to notice," I said with a you-caught-me sigh. "Yeah, I had a bit of a moment mid-death. But hey, the play *is* a tragedy—a little added melodrama can't hurt, right?"

He stepped closer, his expression serious, and my breathing sped up. "Do you want to talk about it?" he asked.

I shook my head. "Not right now."

"Well, you know I'm here."

I looked up into his dark, trusting eyes. "I know." And then, before I could talk myself out of it, I raised myself up on tippy-toes and kissed him. He gasped in surprise but recovered quickly and pulled me closer to him, kissing me back.

He tasted like Chapstick and orange Tic-Tacs, and there was not one iota of fear or doubt in his entire body.

Entirely too soon, the stage door opened and throngs of hyped-up drama kids poured out. Evan and I pulled apart, matching perma-grins on our faces.

"I have to go take care of something," I said regretfully. I didn't want to leave him, but time was of the essence. I may have already been too late. "Don't leave, okay?"

"Never," he promised.

• • •

I weaved through the crowded lobby, searching. I spotted my dads mingling with Roxie and my support group supporters over by the coffee table, but I ran past them with my head down. I would talk to them later. Right now I had to find the principal. He always made a point of coming to the drama productions' opening nights, so he had to be here somewhere. Unless he'd already left. I was really hoping that wasn't the case, because if I had to wait until Monday to tell him my idea, I might lose my nerve.

Finally I saw him chatting with a few teachers, his rolled-up program sticking out of his jacket pocket.

"Excuse me, Mr. Fisher?" I said, tapping him on the shoulder. "Can I speak with you for a minute?"

Shock crossed his face. "Miss Moore! Um…yes, of course! Shall we step into my office?" I followed him as he unlocked the office door and invited me inside. "What can I do for you, Miss Moore?" He pushed his glasses up on his nose nervously.

I smiled. The man was terrified of me. Probably thought I was going to follow through on my lawsuit threat. I should have strung him along for a little while and let him swelter in his wildest fears, but I was eager to get this over with so I could go back to having fun.

"I have a proposition for you," I said, and explained my plan.

39
Day By Day

"Did it start yet?" Dad asked worriedly, hurrying into the living room armed with snacks.

"Not yet. They said seven-oh-eight, so we have a few more minutes," I said. I raised an eyebrow at the colossal popcorn bowl. "You do know it's only a sixty-second commercial, right?"

"So I'm excited. Sue me. It's not every day my daughter is on national television," Dad said.

"I agree, Adam," Evan piped up and helped himself to a giant handful of the buttery stuff. "This occasion absolutely calls for popcorn," he said through a full mouth.

"We third that!" Papa said from the big red armchair, bouncing my little sister on his lap.

I rolled my eyes at the four of them, but I was secretly loving every second of this. I'd already seen the completed commercial, and I was incredibly proud of the way it had turned out. But Dad, Papa, and Evan had insisted on waiting until it aired to watch it—claiming it was more fun knowing they were watching it along with the rest of the country. Or, at least, the percentage of the country who tuned in to *Jeopardy!* at seven p.m. every night.

"Shhhh!" Papa said, as the show cut to commercial. "It's starting!"

I didn't pay much attention to my face on the screen. Instead, I took the full sixty seconds to observe my family as they watched, their faces full of pride and joy.

In the four months since *Romeo and Juliet* closed, I'd come to appreciate exactly how lucky I really was.

• • •

Mr. Fisher had turned out to be an incredibly useful ally in my mission to open the eyes of my peers. As I'd lain fake-bleeding to death on the *Romeo and Juliet* stage back in December, I'd realized that I had to do something. The HIV/AIDS plague wasn't going away, and yet no one was really talking about it. At least, not in the same way they had a decade or two ago. We'd become complacent and we'd become ignorant. Dedicating a health class here or there to discussing statistics and the ways you could and couldn't contract the virus clearly wasn't doing much. If it was, Evan wouldn't have been wary of touching me back when he'd first learned the truth. If it was, Elyse wouldn't have been worried about having caught it through kissing. If it was, I wouldn't be in this situation in the first place.

We needed to talk about it, so that kids would understand that the plague was still spreading across every single demographic— including our own. There needed to be an unrelenting, ongoing discussion so that HIV/AIDS would no longer be this phantom, ghoulish hypothetical and instead be understood as *everyone's* problem—something that we *all* need to be fighting, positive or not. And for the people who were already positive, people like me, we needed to stop the rampant discrimination and judgment in our schools and workplaces and families. The only way to do that? *Keep talking about it.*

So, as my dead body rested on the stage floor that night, I'd asked myself what I could do. I still wasn't comfortable with the assembly idea, and I wasn't the preaching, happy-go-lucky, let's-start-a-student-club type. But there *was* something I was good at.

Mr. Fisher and I approached Andre together.

"Lucy has come to me with a rather intriguing idea," Mr. Fisher said, "and I'd appreciate your full cooperation."

Andre narrowed his eyes at me in suspicion. "What idea?"

"I think we should do another straight play this spring," I said simply.

Andre guffawed. "No way," he said, shaking his head vehemently. "We always do a musical in the spring. It's our biggest moneymaker of the year."

"True. But Mr. Fisher and I have been talking, and we agree that we should do a show that has the ability to truly change our audience's lives. Or, at the very least, make them think. Isn't that the real purpose of theater, after all?" I challenged.

"Of course," Andre mumbled, knowing he couldn't very well

disagree with that. "That's why I chose *The Sound of Music*. What makes you think more than Nazis?"

"*The Normal Heart*," I said without missing a beat.

Andre quickly looked to Mr. Fisher. I could see the possibilities turning in his head and tried to hide my smile. We had him.

"The school would really let us do *The Normal Heart*?" he asked, cautiously optimistic, *The Sound of Music* all but abandoned.

Mr. Fisher nodded. "Lucy has been kind enough to lend me a copy of the play, and though there is some…questionable language involved, I think the overall message is important enough that the school board will overlook the standing no-profanity rule. Just this once," he added.

Andre's face lit up, as the rare chance to do gritty, contemporary theater grew real. "Screw the musical!" he said with a conspiritorial grin.

As was his way, Andre played with casting so that the normally almost all-male play included a few women as well. It was an extremely brutal and challenging show, in my opinion even more of a tragedy than *Romeo and Juliet*. Set in New York City in the very early years of the AIDS crisis, before anyone even had a name for the mysterious disease that was killing so many gay men, the play tackled the very issues I wanted my classmates to be thinking about.

The cast had really stepped up and so far rehearsals were going brilliantly. Every day, I thanked my lucky stars that I lived in a community that was willing to let us do a play like this, and that the administration had such faith in our ability to pull it off.

It was a smaller cast than *Romeo and Juliet*, but all the central people in my life were in it. Evan, Max, Courtney, Ty, Elyse. It was scary at first, working on a project like this with them, when so many of them knew what I was going through and how close to home it rested with me. But I think that made them work even harder, like they didn't want to let me down.

And as far as I could tell, Elyse had kept my secret from Ty. I was impressed, especially considering the fact that we were doing a show about AIDS and it would have been so easy for her to accidentally-on-purpose let it slip at any time. But she was keeping her word. So far, anyway. She and I would never be friends, but at least our feelings toward each other had evolved past sheer hatred and were hovering a little closer to tolerance. I considered that progress.

• • •

The commercial ended, and suddenly my family was pulling me to my feet for a deluge of hugs and kisses. I radiated with accomplishment—I was finally, officially, a professional actor. I had to admit, it felt good.

All at once my cell phone started chirping, and for a while I was busy fielding calls and texts from a gushing Max and Courtney, telling me again how amazing the commercial was—even though I'd already shown them my DVD copy. Then my dads started getting calls from my grandparents and their friends from work, so I took the baby and let them do the proud-parent thing while Evan and I went and sat on the stoop out front. The April air was warm, and the trees were beginning to blossom.

"You're going to be a star," he murmured in my ear. I turned my face to his and answered him with a deep kiss.

"I love you," I whispered, my eyes still closed and my lips still grazing against his. I felt his mouth curl into a smile.

We still hadn't had sex, but we weren't in any rush. Sex complicated things, especially in our case, and after Evan's HIV test had come back negative, neither of us was particularly eager to go down that road again. So, for now, we were perfectly content taking it slow.

I rested my head on his shoulder and readjusted my sleeping baby sister in my arms. She was the mellowest, happiest baby I'd ever seen. I couldn't help but suspect that somehow, she knew what a bullet she'd dodged.

As planned, Lisa had stayed with us until she gave birth. After Papa's virtual in-home imprisonment of her, we all knew she'd be out the door as soon as the baby was born, but what I never could have predicted was that she would leave the baby with us. My dads told me later, though, that they'd known it was a possibility for a while. Lisa asking me to name the baby was the red flag.

I don't know how she looked at that gorgeous, tiny, healthy baby girl and saw anything other than perfection, but Lisa took one look at her and freaked, just as she had with me time and time again. I finally came to realize that it wasn't me that wasn't good enough; it was *her*. She would never be a mother, and she knew it.

I thought about it a lot, and my theory was that all Lisa really wanted was someone to love her. But when her drug addiction and severe lack of any form of compassion prevented that, she decided she would have a baby. In her mind, her baby would love her, no matter what. And who knows, that may have been true. But the variable in the equation was Lisa. After she gave birth, it became clear that she simply wasn't capable of loving the baby in return. And that posed a problem.

So Dad and Papa adopted her, and I finally gave her a name. Viola Freeman-Moore. She'd only been in the world a month and already it was impossible to imagine life without her.

• • •

After dinner, I walked Evan to his car.

"I'll call you later," he promised, and kissed me good-bye.

I watched his taillights disappear around the corner, and then looked down at the object in my hands. A stamped envelope, addressed to Lee Harrison, 177 Spring Street, Apt. 5B, New York, NY, 10012.

Inside was a single sheet of hot pink paper: a schedule for Roxie's meetings. I slid it into the empty mailbox and flipped the little flag up.

Maybe Lee would never show up, but maybe he would. And if he did, we would be there to help him. Because, when it comes down to it, life really isn't all that bad.

And of that I was absolutely positive.

HIV/AIDS at a Glance

What is HIV?

The human immunodeficiency virus (HIV) is a condition that breaks down the immune system so that the body is unable to fight off harmful diseases and infections. The virus is contracted via the sharing of bodily fluids including semen, vaginal fluids, blood, and breast milk.

What is AIDS?

Acquired immunodeficiency syndrome (AIDS) is the most advanced stage of HIV. Since HIV is the virus that initially infects the body, not everyone with HIV has AIDS, but everyone with AIDS has HIV.

Is there a cure?

There is currently no cure or vaccine for HIV or AIDS. However, early testing, care, and treatment (such as medication) can greatly slow the progression of the virus.

Where did HIV and AIDS come from?

Though no one knows the exact cause, genetic research indicates that HIV originated in Africa during the early 1900s. AIDS was first recognized in 1981 and has caused an estimated 30 million deaths (as of 2009). As of 2010, approximately 34 million people around the world are living with HIV.

Facts and Figures

- Though teenagers make up only 25 percent of the sexually active population, they account for nearly half (50 percent) of new sexually transmitted infection (STI) cases.
- Over 61,000 young people (ages 13–29) were estimated to be living with HIV in the U.S. in 2007.
- Young people (ages 13–29) accounted for 39 percent of all *new* HIV cases in the U.S. in 2009 (an extremely high percentage, considering the 15–29 age group makes up only 21 percent of the general U.S. population).
- Most young people with HIV/AIDS were infected via sexual contact.
- Nearly half (46 percent) of all high school students report having had sex.
- Twenty-six percent of female teens and 29 percent of male teens report having had more than one sexual partner.
- Twenty-two percent of teenagers reported using alcohol or drugs during their most recent sexual encounter.

- Thirty-nine percent of teens reported not using a condom during their most recent sexual encounter.

*Information collected from Gay Men's Health Crisis, the Centers for Disease Control and Prevention, and the Kaiser Family Foundation.

HIV/AIDS Resources for Teens

Adolescent AIDS Program offers an extensive list of local HIV/AIDS counseling and testing services for young people around the United States.

- http://www.adolescentaids.org/youth/resource _nationwide.html

MTV's *It's Your (Sex) Life* website is an excellent resource for all things related to teen sexuality, including information on HIV/AIDS (and other STIs), teen pregnancy, and relationships.

- http://www.itsyoursexlife.com

Planned Parenthood has a comprehensive website as well as over 800 health centers around the United States. They are readily available to answer questions and provide quality, nonjudgmental testing and care.

- http://www.plannedparenthood.org/info-for-teens/
- 800-230-PLAN

Gay Men's Health Crisis (GMHC) is "the world's first and leading provider of HIV/AIDS prevention, care, and advocacy." Based in New York City, they offer free testing, counseling, group meetings, healthcare, legal services, and youth programs. If you are not near NYC, you can utilize their website and hotline to find out about testing locations and services in your area.

- http://www.gmhc.org
- 800-243-7692

The Centers for Disease Control and Prevention (CDC) is a wealth of information for up-to-date HIV/AIDS information (including the latest statistics). An entire section of their website is dedicated to HIV/AIDS resources for youth, and they also run a national AIDS hotline (open seven days a week, twenty-four hours a day) that can answer any questions you may have and direct you to a nearby testing site.

- http://www.cdc.gov/hiv/youth/resources.htm
- 800-342-AIDS

An in-home HIV test (similar to an in-home pregnancy test) is also newly available for purchase at drug stores. Approved by the FDA in July 2012, the test consists of an oral swab that produces results in as little as twenty minutes.

Reader Discussion Guide

1.   What do you think of the way Lucy reacts to the problems she faces at the start of the book? How do you think you would react to experiencing a similar string of bad days?

2.   Discuss the role of theater in the book. How does Lucy's love of theater help or hurt her throughout her journey?

3.   When the lab technician Marie asks Lucy how she thinks she will react to a positive HIV result, Lucy doesn't know how to answer. What do you think your response would be to the same question?

4.   Think about the settings of the book. High school drama club, a progressive suburb, New York City. Do you think Lucy's experience with HIV would have been different if she were from a different place or hung out in a different crowd? How so?

5.   How does Lucy's relationship with her fathers change throughout the book? What do you think of her fathers' differing reactions to the news that their daughter has contracted HIV?

6. Do you agree with June that Lucy's impulse to "run away" was learned from watching her absentee mother? Why or why not?

7. Even after taking health and sex education classes in school, Lucy and her friends are still pretty misinformed about the facts surrounding HIV/AIDS. Do you think you're more informed about the subject than they were? Or, like Lucy and Evan, would you also have to do a lot of research in order to educate yourself about the virus? What more can be done to educate teens about HIV/AIDS?

8. Do you think Lucy should have done the "personal responsibility" assembly that her principal asked her to do? Why or why not?

9. Discuss Lucy's relationship with Evan. Is Evan's reaction to the news that his girlfriend has HIV understandable? If not, what should he have done differently?

10. Think about Lucy's friendships with Max, Courtney, and Roxie. If you were Lucy's friend, how would you help her through her challenging journey with HIV?

11. What do you think Lucy's life will be like ten years after the book ends?

Acknowledgments

Like Lucy, for most of my teen years, I dreamed of someday getting to give a Tony Award acceptance speech, where I would laugh and cry and thank everyone who helped me along the way. So here goes—my literary Tony speech. I'll try to keep it short and sweet, before they start playing the music.

First and foremost, to my rock star agent Kate McKean, thank you for taking a chance on me and believing in Lucy's story as much as I do. I wouldn't be here without you.

To the incredibly awesome Sourcebooks Fire team: my amazing editor Leah Hultenschmidt, Aubrey Poole, and Kimberly Manley. Thank you so much for reading this story, loving this story, and working so hard to bring this story to the world. To Katie Casper, thank you for all your hard work on my beautiful cover.

To my friends Colleen and Michael, I'm still waiting for both of you to write those memoirs you've promised me. So get crackin', homies.

To my family, Susan Verdi-Miller, Jim Verdi, and Robert Verdi, thank you for a lifetime of constant love and support, even during those moments where I may have lost my footing a bit.

To Paul Bausch, you're the coolest, raddest, most awesomesauce husband ever. What more can I say? I love you.

To The New School Writing for Children Class of 2012—Alyson, Amber, Caela, Jane, Kevin, Riddhi, and Sona—you are the *best*. Special shout-outs to my beta readers, Dhonielle Clayton, Corey Ann Haydu, and Mary G. Thompson—you guys rock. To my creative writing instructor Tor Seidler, thank you for encouraging me to keep going with this story.

And finally, to Amy Ewing. "Thank you" doesn't do it justice. I could not have written this book—or any of my books—without you. You are the best friend, critique partner, cheerleader, and wine-drinking *Vampire Diaries* viewing buddy a girl could ask for. I'm so lucky to get to be your friend.

About the Author

Jessica Verdi lives in Brooklyn, NY, and received her MFA in Writing for Children from The New School. Her favorite pastimes include singing show tunes at the top of her lungs (much to her husband's chagrin), watching cheesy TV, and scoring awesome nonleather shoes in a size 5. She's still trying to figure out a way to put her uncanny ability to remember both song lyrics and the intricacies of vampire lore to good use. Follow Jess on Twitter @jessverdi.